MICHAEL FUTCHER is a director, writer, dramaturg and actor. Over the last thirty years he has worked with all the major Queensland theatre companies in various capacities, has conducted national tours of several major works, and has appeared on screen in Australia and UK.

HELEN HOWARD is an actor, writer, director, acting and accent coach for stage and screen. Since settling in Brisbane in 1994, she has performed with Queensland's leading theatre companies as an actor, and worked on several major feature films and tv series in her coaching capacity.

Their writing collaborations include *1001 Nights* (2013, Zen Zen Zo/QTC/Qld Music Festival), *Therese Raquin* (2012, Zen Zen Zo), *Treasure Island* (2011, national tour with Matrix/QTC), *The Wishing Well* (2008, Matrix/La Boite, Currency Press), *The Drowning Bride* (2005, Matilda Award Winner, shortlisted for the Qld Premier's Literary Awards, Currency Press), *Citizen Jane* (2002, Qld Arts Council, Playlab Press), *Cutting Loose* (2000, Matrix Theatre), *1347* (1996, Matrix Theatre), *The King And The Corpse!* (1995, Matilda Award Winner, Playlab Press), *Disobediently Yours Edmund Kean* (1992, London Fringe). *A Beautiful Life* has won a Matilda Award, and was shortlisted for the Qld Premier's Literary Awards and for a Green Room Award, as well as being nominated for an AWGIE Award. As a solo writer Helen has also written *Talking Dirty* (2006, as part of *Sex Cubed* for La Boite), and *Beetle-Eyed* (2011, Griffith University). In 2009, Helen and Michael received the Playlab award for their outstanding contribution to Queensland Theatre.

They have run their own theatre company, Matrix Theatre, since 1994, and live in Brisbane with their two sons Frankie and Jimmy.

A Beautiful Life

MICHAEL FUTCHER AND HELEN HOWARD

CURRENCY PRESS
SYDNEY

CURRENCY PLAYS

First published in 2000
by Currency Press Pty Ltd
PO Box 2287, Strawberry Hills, NSW, 2012, Australia
enquiries@currency.com.au
www.currency.com.au

Reprinted 2005, 2009, 2010, 2013, 2015, 2016, 2018

Copyright © Michael Futcher and Helen Howard, 2000

The moral rights of the authors have been asserted.

NATIONAL LIBRARY OF AUSTRALIA CIP DATA

Author:	Futcher, Michael, 1964–
Title:	A beautiful life.
ISBN:	9780868196053 (paperback)
	I. Howard, Helen, 1962–.
	II. Title.
Dewey Number:	A822.3

Typeset by Paul O'Beirne for Currency Press.
Cover design by Katy Wall for Currency Press.
Front cover shows Yalin Ozucelik as Amir in the 1998 Matrix Theatre company production (photo Rob Maccoll).

Currency Press acknowledges the Traditional Owners of the Country on which we live and work. We pay our respects to all Aboriginal and Torres Strait Islander Elders, past and present.

Contents

Dedicated to Mohammad, Laleh, Ali and Parisa

FOREWORD

My initial encounter with *A Beautiful Life* was by way of a first draft that had been written after a creative development workshop and had already been given a public reading. The response to the reading had been enthusiastic. Helen Howard and Michael Futcher were encouraged to develop the script further and to take it on to a full production.

I had worked with Helen and Michael as actors and I was familiar with Matrix Theatre's earlier work—a physical, highly theatrical form of storytelling, incorporating stylised movement and direct address to the audience. Their work evolves through improvisation with the actors and the performances are disciplined, exciting to watch and lots of fun. My only knowledge of *A Beautiful Life* was that it was based on the life story of an Iranian musician who'd worked with Matrix. It is to Helen's and Michael's credit that not only did they immediately recognise the theatrical potential of his story but they made of it a genuine drama.

On reading the first draft I was struck by Helen's and Michael's passion to tell what is an extraordinary story of an ordinary man, whom they called Hamid, and his struggle against a cruel and repressive regime. How an act of kindness giving shelter to a friend in need leads to years of incarceration and torture. How another act of kindness, rescuing a family of Australian tourists from the clutches of a belligerent militia, leads to his family escaping from Iran and being granted asylum in Australia. How his quiet, beautiful life in Australia is turned upside down when a peaceful protest at the Iranian Embassy in Canberra turns nasty and he's labelled a terrorist. How the political will of the Australian Government is wielded against him through the legal system so that an important trading partner might be appeased. How exercising his right to speak in an Australian court about the murder, cruelty and torture, the whole sorry history of human rights abuses by the Iranian Government, lands him in an Australian gaol for a year. How by speaking out he risked deportation to Iran and certain death when silence might have earned him a suspended sentence.

It is the story of repeated acts of heroism, not the heroism of defiance but the heroism required to do what one believes is right despite the consequences. The right to speak, the right to natural justice. And to continue to live by these principles, acting on them time and time again. Yet Hamid is an ordinary, quite simple man caught up in events too big to comprehend, way beyond his control. He doesn't think of himself as a hero, he simply does what he believes to be right. It is this selfless, unconscious heroism that shines through the script from the first draft to the present, that informed and inspired its creation and continues to inspire its performance. This and Helen's and Michael's belief that here was a story that begged and deserved to be told, a very human story that graphically exposed the chasm that can exist between law and justice.

Because I had not been involved in the development and writing process I was able to read the first draft, not as a faithful account of a real life, but as a work of constructed drama. That the actual events are compelling, emotionally powerful and inherently dramatic, does not mean they, of themselves, will make a good play. Like sow's ears, plays have a habit of being what they are and no amount of development and rewriting can supply that all important theatrical spark if it's not there. Already present in the first draft were the essential ingredients and conventions that would make the performance text a success. The important events of Hamid's and his wife Jhila's life in Iran were framed by the Embassy protest at the beginning and the subsequent trial and sentencing at the end. Interspersed in the present were scenes where his lawyers, the fictional Brendan and Stephanie, build the case for his defence as well as the sub-plot of their romance. Hamid's and Jhila's son, Amir, provides ironic narrative links and there are the characteristic Matrix performance trademarks of storytelling through physical action in the prison scenes and Hamid's escape from Iran. Already the suggestion was there of a rose being passed from scene to scene, increasing in potency as a symbol of beauty, growth and survival.

Helen and Michael were aware that the first draft was largely narrative driven and with this script they were endeavouring to develop Matrix's work to incorporate more elements of drama without sacrificing their theatrical physicality. It was also evident from the reading that there were structural problems. The first half was action-packed, the Embassy protest, legal proceedings, life in Iran, Hamid's capture and torture. The second half was about life in gaol, rescuing the Australians, the adventure of the escape, the trials. The first half was thoroughly engaging, with surprising developments; but the suspense and tension was not maintained in the second half.

The challenge in creating drama is to suggest why something happened, why someone took a particular course of action rather than merely telling or showing what happened or how. Keeping in mind the actual events of the story, using all the existing elements in the script we set about teasing out and constructing the drama by asking 'Why?' of all the characters.

Why doesn't Hamid strike, kill Ahmad when he has the chance at the Embassy? Focusing upon and examining this frozen moment—the spanner raised to strike—became absolutely crucial to the development of the script, not only as part of Hamid's defence in the trial but as the key to understanding him psychologically. Why doesn't he want to kill this man as Kamran tries to do? In a development from the first draft we thought Hamid should actually stop Kamran. By asking and answering these questions Helen and Michael deepened the relationship between Hamid and Kamran. In the early draft Kamran was an incidental character, who appears at the protest and as a devout Muslim caught up in the Iranian prison system. Another character altogether was Hamid's friend in prison. The writers conflated these characters, making Kamran central to Hamid's survival in prison, befriending him and teaching him how to make in his mind a beautiful place, a sanctuary from the provocations and deprivations of prison life. This resolution came about by asking why Hamid feels obligated to look after Kamran in his own home, especially after Kamran accuses Hamid of betraying him. Asking what Hamid, a self-confessed sinner, might learn from the devout Kamran in prison. Asking why, if Kamran could create in his mind 'a miraculous carpet, of intricate beauty', is he now so destroyed? Why does he feel so betrayed? And what part did Hamid play in his destruction?

Ahmad was always involved in Hamid's torture scenes but so far was unnamed. In a new development the writers introduced Ahmad into the Iranian prison scenes as a guard, initially friendly and helpful, but turning vicious when crossed. In asking why Kamran would try to kill Ahmad they began to build a relationship between the two and came up with the power struggle that is played out over the good shoes that Kamran refuses to surrender until the night he offers them up to save Hamid from a beating. Having been saved by Kamran, Hamid then has the opportunity to retrieve the shoes by killing Ahmad; but he doesn't follow through and is forced to watch Kamran being mercilessly tortured. By means of invention, poetic licence, the paths and fates of these three characters are now dramatically interlocked, and the key to unlocking this shadowy past is that frozen moment at the Embassy.

This moment is also pivotal in the case Brendan and Stephanie build in Hamid's defence. Initially they place no great importance on it. Pursuing her own ambitions, Stephanie wants to fight to get the charges dropped. Brendan opts for pragmatism, a limited admission of guilt, believing at worst Hamid, Jhila and Kamran will get off with a fine and a good behaviour bond. When the charges are changed to conspiracy, the lawyers know the case is all but lost unless they can subpoena the diplomats and prove that Ahmad provoked the riot by first leaving the gates open and then by opening the door. In actuality there was never any likelihood of the diplomats appearing in court, even at the outset, and it was from this point that the fiction departed totally from the original scenario. For the sake of the drama, to keep the legal action and Brendan and Stephanie alive, the writers invented this scenario. In the first draft the affair between Brendan and Stephanie, aided by the complication of Brendan's failing marriage, carried almost as much weight as Hamid's defence. Some commentators at the first reading suggested more should be made of them but the writers knew that this would further unbalance Hamid's journey. There was no doubt in their minds that Brendan and Stephanie were there to serve Hamid and his story, not *vice versa*.

The development of the interlocking destinies of Hamid, Kamran and Ahmad had implications for the release of information and now required a restructuring of the play, particularly of the Brendan and Stephanie strand. In the early draft, the lawyers visit to the Embassy came at the end of part one and brought Stephanie and Brendan together. It gave them the focus of pursuing the diplomats who then leave Australia at the eleventh hour, just as the case is about to go to court. In this draft, Brendan tries to build a case against the conspiracy charge by browbeating Hamid about what he can and can't say. Kamran taunts Hamid who clams up, saying that handcuffs are being put on his mouth. Looking for another angle Brendan buys into Stephanie's theory that Ahmad provoked the riot at the Embassy. He then makes an impulsive visit to the Embassy which frightens the diplomats off and puts the whole case in jeopardy. A further consequence of the visit is that it is the catalyst in the breakup of the couple's affair. When her boss threatens Stephanie's position in the firm, she adopts a more pragmatic stance on the defence and betrays Brendan's trust.

In the earlier draft Hamid's press conference was only referred to by the lawyers, but in discussions about the characters and their journeys it seemed important that we see what happened, why the lawyers think Hamid shouldn't be allowed to speak for himself. It also allows a journalist to ask, given the suffering that Hamid is claiming the Iranian regime has caused, why they, and Kamran in particular, hadn't killed anyone. Hamid's self-doubt is voiced by someone completely outside the event and Kamran attacks him. From this moment Hamid is surrounded by torturers—Kamran, Brendan and Stephanie, Amir, even Jhila—all wanting to dig up the past, all with expectations of what he should do in the present, all reminding him of his failings, his secret fears of cowardice with which he tortures himself.

Another quite radical restructuring was brought about by the needs of Hamid's emotional arc over the whole play. People loved the playfulness and theatricality of the recounting of his rescue of the Australians and his escape from Iran. Though these sequences were chronologically in the right place, towards the end of the second part, they had the effect of undercutting the tension. Just as things are beginning to look grim in Australia and in prison, we're enjoying seeing Hamid out of prison and escaping from Iran. He was home free and the drama had to be cranked up again for his trials in Iran and Australia. The writers were loathe to lose this sequence so a new place had to be found for it. We'd questioned: 'Why Amir is the narrator rather than Hamid? What's his relationship with Hamid like? How much does he actually know about the past? Is Amir the narrator because Hamid doesn't want to face those demons again and there are things he is reluctant to tell?' The rescue and escape sequence became a way for Amir to get Hamid to tell his story and to convince Brendan that his father wasn't a bad man, certainly not a terrorist. It proved to be a great contrast to go from the joy and playfulness of this sequence to the darkness and disturbance of the press conference. Sitting where it does now, completely out of time and place, it serves another useful purpose. It introduces the audience to another storytelling convention involving role-playing, several narrators and a kind of shorthand re-enactment of the past. The audience was already familiar with Amir's role as ironic narrator, freezing and commenting on the action. After this sequence we hoped they would be ready to go with everything.

After the chaos of the beginning and having established the sense of wheels turning within wheels, stories living within stories, the play settles down. Amir takes us back to where it all began with Masud, to establish the context for everything that we've seen, and to understand Hamid's plea that all Australians must know what happened in Iran in order to understand what happened here. In the first draft Masud pursues much the same course as he does in the performance version but we were able to tease out the drama, to bring it more forward in the scene so that there was a greater sense of threat and unease. Why has he come here? Why does he risk the lives of his friends? Why does he test them? Why do Hamid and Jhila let him stay? Why does he stay so long? Why does he go? In the first draft he appeared as if from nowhere, almost nonchalantly. Now there is a knock on the door at night, a terrifying thing in Iran, especially if you were caught drinking and dancing, both forbidden by the mullahs. Now when he enters he comes knowing he is being chased. If this is his last refuge can he still trust these people who used to be his friends? If he is much changed after three years might not they be? And how? So he has to test their allegiances by provoking discussion about Khomeni and the Mojahedin. The writers wanted to make more present the danger of his visit and the desperateness of his purpose. Significantly, the story of his sister's rape and execution was transferred from a later scene when he wakes from a bad dream. In the performance version it becomes a way for Masud to warn Hamid and Jhila of the fate that could await them if they take him in, a member of the Mojahedin.

Masud's story is tragic and he dies a hero's death, fully cognisant of the likely outcome of his actions. The consequences of his visit are almost as tragic for Hamid and Jhila and no less heroic. Their lives are changed forever. Ten years on, just as they might rightly expect to settle into a beautiful life, they are swept into the maelstrom again, as the weight of law is used to deny a man and his family natural justice.

I have included these examples as an indication of the sort of work we did on every scene and every character; and also as an indication of how often the solutions found already existed in the first draft. Sometimes they were buried in the text, sometimes in another scene, sometimes contained in the writers' reasons why the text was as it was, sometimes because it was what actually happened. The writers didn't write a different play (plays are what they are), but a clearer version. If they had to bend the truth and at times invent motives and events it was, hopefully, to make a better play that might tell a bigger Truth.

It all sounds simple in retrospect, perhaps even obvious, but it took a year, a series of meetings, to talk through and challenge the actions and motivations of the characters, aided by some significant restructuring. All of this was done with notes over dinners and bottles of wine while a baby crawled on the floor. Scenes written up on cards were shuffled around on a pin board. Another draft was written, another reading, more meetings, more dinners, more questions and yet another draft to take into rehearsals. And there the refining process continued until the actors cried enough.

What makes this a particularly Australian play? It is set in Australia now and in the past, in the minds of Australians. It is about Australia as much as it is about Iran. The intercutting of the trial scenes in Australia and Iran invites us to take the easy option and draw the conclusion that our system of law and justice is no better than that in Iran. We feel vindicated in siding with the put-upon Hamid, declaring our law an ass and justice an illusion. In the very next scene Hamid, with typical humility, dismantles our taking this privileged position. He knows he and his family are better off here. He knows he was guilty of property damage and he knows how to survive in gaol. Kamran taught him well. Most importantly he had his day in court, exercised his right to speak, his one small victory, and for now it's enough.

What seems difficult for Australia to accept is that there is, and can be, no forgetting of the past by the peoples it accepts as migrants and refugees. We don't want to know their stories. Worse, we expect them to be silent. In wanting to silence them we are all complicit in the misfortunes that befell them. As Masud and various sages through the ages have said, 'In silence lies obedience'. And approval, when the best service we could provide is to listen. By listening, acknowledge them. Listen and then consider, quietly and simply, what is the right thing to do.

Janis Balodis
Goonellabah
May, 2000

AUTHORS' INTRODUCTION

A Beautiful Life began its gestation on a chill night in July 1995. It was the final performance of *The King and the Corpse!*, an outdoor production in the Mount Coot-tha Botanical Gardens, and as we packed up the set, one of our musicians approached us. He was an Iranian, whom we'd come to respect as a talented and committed member of our cast, but about whom we knew little else. He told us, with great humility, that he wanted to tell his life story and that he wished Matrix (our theatre company) to be the instrument through which it might reach the public. With a sense of trepidation (for we feared that his story might be dull) mixed with excitement (for in our bones we knew it would not be) we joined our new friend and his family for a sumptuous Iranian feast of food and storytelling. We were not disappointed. While our friend regarded this sharing of his story as something of a cathartic experience, we have never seen his confidence in us as anything but an act of great friendship and generosity. Friendship takes on a new depth of meaning within the Iranian context, as the play reveals, and ours with 'Hamid' and 'Jhila' has deepened with the work which followed that night's revelations.

The Australia Council funded an initial workshop period with three actors to explore our material through improvisation. This followed many hours of recorded conversation with our friends—Hamid's contribution always finding the humorous vein within tragedy, his tenuous but gritty hold on the English language making for imaginative expression, whilst Jhila's quick mind, grappling with an unfamiliar tongue, found the sharpest single word to hone his meaning—through which we built a picture of their struggle to escape persecution and injustice. The potential for theatrical treatment of this material was already huge; against a backdrop of adventure rupturing ordinary lives were moments of pure comedy, moments of horror, and a vision of personal growth for Hamid and Jhila accelerated to Jack and the Beanstalk proportions. Our actors, David Brown, Siobhan Lawless and Vince Atkinson, gamely tackled the improvisations in spite of the complex 'notes' we'd prepared, and helped us immeasurably to see the possibilities for bringing the story to theatrical life, and a direction for the writing to come. Much of their work has been retained in the final script, for which we are indebted to them.

However, it was not until Hamid and Jhila insisted we watch a documentary made by Barbara Chobocky, and screened by SBS, that we began to realise just how relevant this nascent work might be to our society. The documentary followed the fortunes of a group of Iranian refugees who had joined together on the spur of the moment to protest outside the Iranian Embassy in Canberra. Like fellow Iranians the world over, they were horrified by the news that many Mojahedin members (Iranian freedom fighters) had been bombed by Iranian government forces and killed. They flocked to embassies within their new countries to draw attention to Iran's actions and to demand that trade sanctions be imposed. In Canberra, the protest finished in an invasion of the building and a seven-minute attack on pictures, documents and filing cabinets, with one official receiving a head wound requiring hospital treatment. Barbara Chobocky's *The Raid* used footage of the protest captured by an SBS news crew who had been alerted to the event by the protesters themselves. By examining in detail this footage she revealed the superficial nature of the 'violence', and by interviewing the perpetrators she showed them to be naïve, ordinary people desperate to pick up the pieces of their new lives in Australia, but now haunted by an act which branded them 'terrorists' in the media, lost some of them their livelihoods and, in some cases, their freedom. In the rest of the world, the similar offences committed at other embassies were dealt with swiftly, with minimal sentencing; in Australia, the court case lasted almost two years and resulted in several long jail terms. On learning this, we set about weaving into the plot the story of the raid, which brought a pertinence and resonance to the play for Australian audiences, and the lawyers became our means to examine reactions amongst Australians to the 'terrorists'. It also allowed us to interweave two trial scenes: one in the Iranian jail, where Hamid was beaten and gagged; the other in Australia, where the judge forbade the jury to take into account any evidence supplied by Hamid about his terrible history, which might have encouraged them to feel empathy with him and his fellow defendants.

There followed a period of intense writing, culminating in a public reading of a first draft version of the play at La Boite Theatre with professional actors. Although a harrowing experience—having to expose a first draft script to public discussion—it showed us that others found the tale gripping and important. Not least amongst these others were John Kotzas (representing the Energex Brisbane Festival) and Sue Rider (Artistic Director of La Boite Theatre) whose enthusiasm led to their organisations' involvement as co-producers with Matrix (already funded by Arts Queensland and the Australia Council) during which time we were grateful for their advice and feedback. With this kind of support, we were able, suddenly, to invite into the process its most valuable element—Janis Balodis. In what became an exciting and inspiring relationship, it was his dramaturgical advice which allowed us to discover the deeper resonance in the story; he encouraged us to cut and juxtapose scenes in such a way that the dramatic tension was maintained until the end, whilst preserving the spirit of the piece.

Writers as directors might sound like a recipe for disaster to some, but in our case it allowed us to stay one step ahead of the process, and to develop images which had been forming in our minds during the writing. Often our initial ideas for bringing difficult scenes to life seemed outlandish and impossible to our talented cast, but their willingness to try anything once, and sometimes a hundred times, was to their credit. Throughout the writing process we had been aware that a visceral, theatrical style of playing would be essential to the play's success, and the rehearsal period served to confirm that knowledge. The many challenges for the actors included the realisation of the inhuman prison scenes, and the escape scene with its image of thirteen escapees packed into a ute speeding across the desert. The answer lay in developing movements which revealed the essence of the required actions rather than a naturalistic representation of them. For instance, the dread and excitement of the ute journey was revealed through the actors rhythmically clapping in counter-point to Amir's narration, whilst packed impossibly onto a coffin-sized metal cage. In general, the actors changed character, the action changed location and the dialogue became narration in an instant. The pace was fast with hardly a beat to separate scenes. The whole play seemed to move along with the energy of Amir's determination that his father's story be told.

Since the co-production with La Boite and the Energex Brisbane Festival of 1998, we have had a chance to examine the script more objectively, and have managed to make a few small cuts here and there, but essentially it remains intact. Performance is the greatest test for a play, and *A Beautiful Life* grows when brought to the stage. The production was highly acclaimed, and appreciated by its audiences during the Festival, but for us the most important measure of its success was in the judgement of Hamid and Jhila, who found that it remained true to their story, even after our efforts to adapt it for the theatre, and delighted in seeing people come away enlightened and moved by their experiences. Most of those people never realised that the subject of the piece, Hamid himself, was playing with the musicians in their semi-shrouded gallery above the action, and that his passionate applause for the actors at the end of each performance was augmented by his euphoria at finding a voice in his new land.

We are immensely grateful to all those who helped Matrix realise the dream of telling Hamid's and Jhila's story, particularly: Barbara Chobocky, Janis Balodis, David Brown, Sue Rider, Bill Haycock, Jenni Kubler and Tony Auckland (and all at KAM), John and Kathleen Futcher, Marian and Gordon Leak, our cast and musicians, and to Wendy Blacklock at Performing Lines for facilitating the national tour for 2000.

Michael Futcher and Helen Howard
Brisbane, May 2000

DISCLAIMER

A Beautiful Life is based on the reminiscences of an Iranian refugee and his wife who settled in Australia in the late 1980s; and on the experiences of other refugees involved in an actual raid on the Iranian Embassy in Canberra in 1992, as reported in newspapers and on television.

The Iranian history of the character 'Ahmad' was created for the play as a fictional composite of several 'real-life' personalities and types and should not be seen to represent any particular individual, living or dead, and who may have been present at the Embassy when the raid took place.

The true events on which the play is based have been interpreted in a dramatic way and, therefore, *A Beautiful Life* should not be regarded as representing historical fact.

*Angelina Quick as Jhila and Eugene Gilfedder as Hamid in the
1998 Matrix Theatre Company production at the La Boite Theatre,
Brisbane. (Photo: Rob Maccoll)*

A Beautiful Life was first performed by Matrix Theatre Company, as a co-production with La Boite and the Energex Brisbane Festival, at La Boite Theatre on 27 August 1998 with the following cast:

HAMID	Eugene Gilfedder
JHILA	Angelina Quick
AMIR	Yalin Ozucelik
AHMAD	Russell Dykstra
STEPHANIE / NEDA /PENNY	Caroline Kennison
BRENDAN / JAMES	Joss McWilliam
HAMAD'S FATHER / KAMRAN / INTERROGATOR / MR DARABI / MULLAH	Errol O'Neill
MASUD / REZA / HOHN JUDGE	Sandro Colarelli

PROTESTORS, PROSECUTOR, WOMAN, REMAND CENTRE GUARDS, LAWYERS, ISLAMIC REVOLUTIONARY GUARDS, JEWS, DRIVER, SMUGGLER, JOURNALISTS, HAMID'S FAMILY and PRISONERS were played by members of the company.

Director, Michael Futcher
Assistant Director, Helen Howard
Dramaturgical Assistance, Janis Balodis
Designer, Bill Haycock
Lighting Designer, Matt Scott
Music performed by Francis Gilfedder, Roland Adeney and Cieavash Arean

PRODUCTION NOTE

As writers and co-creators of *A Beautiful Life*, Michael Futcher and Helen Howard, who comprise Matrix Theatre, allowed the conventions required to perform the piece to evolve organically as they worked with the actors.

It is essential that the same actor plays Amir at all ages within the play; nearly three years old in Iran, about thirteen at the time of the protest (although he exaggerates his age in some scenes), and about nineteen in the present (1998) as the narrator. As a three-year-old, Amir is 'mimed' by the other actors, while the adult actor speaks for him. All the actors take on multiple characters within the play, except Hamid, and it is suggested that the actor playing Jhila portrays only non-speaking characters such as prisoners, and that Amir only plays other roles in the Iranian, not the Australian, reality.

Please note no actual Farsi is spoken in the play. When it is indicated in the text that the Iranian characters would be speaking in their native Farsi amongst themselves, it is important that the actors speak fluently in the actor's own neutral accent. When they speak English it is hesitant and they use a Farsi accent. Hamid is more comfortable with English than Jhila, who improves during the play; Amir speaks both English and Farsi with a neutral accent. Within the Australian scenes, where English is spoken most of the time, it has been indicated in the text where the characters are speaking Farsi.

To facilitate the rapid shifts in time and location in the story, costumes and props should be kept to a minimum, and scenes be allowed to flow without pause from one into another, with the eight actors remaining on stage throughout.

A 'chador' is a black cloak worn by women in Iran, all in one piece over other clothes, and is considered an extreme form of 'hejab'—where women wear a scarf, and a long garment over trousers. For the purposes of the first production the chador was represented simply with squares of black material.

CHARACTERS

HAMID PARSI, an Iranian

JHILA, his wife

AMIR, their son

AHMAD HUSSEINI, an Iranian

KAMRAN, an Iranian

STEPHANIE JAMES, an Australian lawyer

BRENDAN O'SULLIVAN, an Australian lawyer

PENNY BOLTON, an Australian

JAMES BOLTON, an Australian

HAMID'S FATHER

REZA AFSHAR, an Iranian

NEDA, AN IRANIAN, Hamid's eldest sister, wife of Reza

MASUD AMINI, an Iranian

MR DARABI

INTERROGATOR

JOHN, an Australian lawyer

MULLAH

JUDGE, an Australian

PROTESTERS, PROSECUTOR, WOMAN, REMAND CENTRE GUARDS, LAWYERS, ISLAMIC REVOLUTIONARY GUARDS, JEWS, DRIVER, SMUGGLER, JOURNALISTS, HAMID'S FAMILY, AND PRISONERS

PROLOGUE

HAMID's voice is heard as JHILA, *swathed in a black chador and holding a rose, emerges from the shadows, between three tall figures also shrouded in black. She is watched by* AMIR, *her son. She cherishes the rose for a moment then lets it drop through a shaft of light, into a pool of water.*

HAMID: I want to tell you a story, my son, a story about yourself.
Just two springs had passed you by, not knowing that you dwelt
In a place on the borders of freedom.
A black demon took your father, just because he loved a friend.
You looked for Daddy everywhere, not knowing where to find the
    jail,
And sang for him in sorrow.
You asked for him from everyone, entreating them to find him,
Your small tongue sweetly tripping, over all the words and
    verbs,
In sweetly ordered sense.

> JHILA *casts the chador aside. She lets down her hair and washes her face in the pool.*

Even to the prison guards: 'Sir, take to Daddy his Amir',
And finding Daddy in your fury, your sweet voice then
    resounded,
Your little heart too full with pain:
'When I come back I will break all the locks,
I will kill all them here and take you.'

> JHILA *rushes to one of the shrouded figures.*

1

ACT ONE

SCENE ONE

The Iranian Embassy, Canberra. April, 1992.

JHILA *rips away the shroud from one of the figures to reveal a coffin-like cage representing a filing cabinet, and smashes it to the ground.*

JHILA: Down with demon Khomeini! Down with demon Khomeini!

> *An eruption of violence. A diplomat,* AHMAD HUSSEINI, *staggers backwards holding a fire extinguisher threateningly at a small, angry mob. One actor carries a hand-held light, signifying a camera, shining it on each major action. The other two shrouded figures are violently stripped and sent crashing to the ground.* HAMID *sprays a large red 'X' on an image of Ayatollah Khomeini. The mob rampages over the scattered documents, setting fire to some.*

ALL: Down with Khomeini! Black demon! Down with regime of Khomeini! Killers of Mojahedin! Enemy of freedom!

> JHILA *throws a bottle of red soft drink at the image of Ayatollah Khomeini. There is chaos.* KAMRAN *enters, lost and disassociated.*

HAMID: [*holding a heavy ring-binder, breathless*] Look. Thirty-five thousand political prisoners held in Iran. All in here.

PROTESTER ONE: Show the camera!

> HAMID *shows the binder to the actor with the light.*

HAMID: Thirty-five thousand political prisoners in Iranian jail, dying—these are faces of the dead. Viva human rights!

PROTESTER ONE: Camera, follow me!

> *The light follows him as* AHMAD *throws a wastepaper bin, narrowly missing* HAMID.

Down with the regime of Khomeini!

The light remains on PROTESTER ONE *as he searches for photographs, while away from the light* AHMAD *lunges at* HAMID *to grab the binder.* HAMID *raises a spanner over his head. There is a moment of recognition.* AHMAD *steps back. They stare.* KAMRAN *lunges at* AHMAD *with a screwdriver. The camera light swings onto* HAMID *as he moves forward towards* AHMAD *and* KAMRAN, *still with the spanner raised. The action freezes.*

AMIR: I come home after two days away to an empty house, so I turn the television on for company. There are these men and women in white overalls surrounded by police, and they catch my eye because they look Iranian. The man on the news says they were arrested for raiding the Iranian Embassy in Canberra, that they're terrorists. But they look more like lost astronauts. Like they've flown in from another planet. They show film of them doing it, and when it stops there's this man holding a spanner in the air. [*Pause.*] It's my dad!

PROTESTER ONE: [*breaking the freeze*] Camera here! Closer! Victims of torture. [*Showing the camera a photograph of a torture victim*] See!

HAMID *breaks his freeze and grabs* KAMRAN. AHMAD *is bleeding.* KAMRAN *wields the screwdriver, trying to kill* AHMAD. HAMID *grabs his arm and stops him.*

HAMID: [*in Farsi—see Production Note, page xxiii regarding accent*] No!

KAMRAN: [*to* HAMID, *in Farsi*] Why?

HAMID: [*to a* PROTESTER, *in Farsi*] Get him out of here!

KAMRAN *is dragged away. The* PROTESTERS *disperse.* AHMAD *and* HAMID *stare at one another.*

JHILA: [*in Farsi*] Hamid! Let's go. Hamid—come on! Hamid!

They exit.

AHMAD: [*in Farsi*] You're finished! [*He touches the blood on his head then falls to his knees. In English*] Agh—God—bashed! I am bashed! [*He reaches for his handkerchief, folds it into a pad and goes to apply it to his head, but stops and replaces it in his top pocket.*] Hey you, cameraperson. Look, blood—terrorists! Mojahedin terrorists did this—come back—you film blood—come back!

He exits. The disrupted stage is empty as voices from offstage call out in Farsi.

PROTESTER ONE: [*offstage*] Kamran!
PROTESTER TWO: [*offstage*] Kamran—where are you? Come on!
PROTESTER ONE: [*offstage*] Kamran!
PROTESTER TWO: [*offstage*] Let's get out of here.

KAMRAN *enters. He stops in a garden, delighted with it, and wanders through some rose bushes, smelling their scent. He picks the rose from the pool. A* WOMAN *emerges from the house.*

WOMAN: What are you doing in my garden?

KAMRAN *holds out the rose.*

You! This is private property. I'll call the police.
KAMRAN: [*approaching the* WOMAN, *in Farsi*] Stop. Don't shoot. Take off that uniform. You're my brother.

KAMRAN *imagines the* WOMAN *to be a soldier and grasps his/her imaginary gun barrel, slotting the rose stem into it. The* WOMAN *takes the rose and* KAMRAN *smiles.*

HAMID: [*running, in Farsi*] He's here! It's all right Kamran. Jhila! [*To the* WOMAN, *in English.*] Excuse me.

JHILA *enters.*

WOMAN: Is he all right?
HAMID: He's fine, thank you. [*In Farsi*] Time to go, Kamran.
KAMRAN: [*to* HAMID, *in Farsi*] You betrayed me…

HAMID *steps back. Their action slows, as* AHMAD *enters showing an unseen group of* REPORTERS *the debris, while Embassy employees clear it up.* AMIR *shines the hand-held light on* AHMAD's *face.*

AHMAD: Ladies and gentlemen, I ask you to be careful. You see how much debris is here. They try to burn down Embassy—
AMIR: Ahmad Husseini, diplomat.
AHMAD: —Maybe small bomb. It is premeditated action by Mojahedin terrorists. Look at what they do. [*He indicates his head.*] They are enemies of Iran. Enemies of Australia.

AMIR: The newspapers are calling it 'Bloody Monday'. They're falling over themselves for the best headline. It's top story on every TV news. Terrorism in Australia.

AHMAD: Even here we are not safe.

AMIR: People are scared—a bunch of Muslim fanatics are running loose in Canberra.

AHMAD: It is unfortunate that Australian Government did not protect us here. However, I thank your Minister of Trade for his apology.

AMIR: Everyone is in shock—we're not used to it here, it's un-Australian. It must be—Mr Keating said so on TV.

AHMAD: Your Prime Minister, he says this is not the kind of violence you are used to here. It is not acceptable. This is good. We must stop this terrorism with tough justice. Thank you.

    A PROSECUTOR*'s voice resounds.*

PROSECUTOR: Our country has separately responded to these people in a sympathetic way by allowing them to come to live in this country, and settle as refugees.

HAMID: [*in Farsi*] Kamran—it's Hamid.

JHILA: [*in Farsi*] He's okay… come on, Kamran.

HAMID: [*to the* WOMAN, *in English*] I'm sorry.

PROSECUTOR: We are allowed to ask for some things in return. We are allowed to ask them not to use their presence here as an opportunity to seek revenge for what happened in their homeland. We are allowed to ask them to leave their national disputes behind them.

    HAMID *and* JHILA *take* KAMRAN *to one side.*

AMIR: He was talking about my mum and dad—the Prosecutor—when they were arrested. How the hell did it happen? I knew they were going down to protest. Just to protest. But they did this thing and now people are saying this is the day Australia lost its innocence. And there I was thinking that happened a couple of hundred years ago.

♦ ♦ ♦ ♦ ♦

SCENE TWO

The Remand Centre, Canberra.

STEPHANIE *gathers papers.* BRENDAN *enters.*

STEPHANIE: Brendan!

BRENDAN: I've got clients waiting.

AMIR: I got the first bus to Canberra and headed for the Remand Centre.

STEPHANIE: Where the hell have you been?

BRENDAN: At a meeting.

STEPHANIE: What meeting?

BRENDAN: A divorce.

STEPHANIE: A divorce?

BRENDAN: It needed my immediate attention.

STEPHANIE: I've just been humiliated by a bloody fascist Magistrate trying to get bail for your clients.

AMIR: Excuse me. Are you Stephanie James?

STEPHANIE: Yes.

AMIR: I'm Amir Parsi.

STEPHANIE: Oh!

AMIR: The policeman on the door said you could take me to my mum and dad.

STEPHANIE: Right. They're in the room at the end of the corridor.

AMIR: Thanks. [*To* BRENDAN] You're the guy who got Darren Jones off that biting charge, aren't you?

STEPHANIE: He's great with footballers.

AMIR: Wait till I tell Mum and Dad who's defending us!

     He goes to HAMID *and* JHILA.

STEPHANIE: [*to* BRENDAN] I just want to make one thing clear—

BRENDAN: Yes Miss?

STEPHANIE: I'm not carrying you through this.

BRENDAN: You won't have to. I'll be out of here as soon as Peter finds someone else.

STEPHANIE: You have a problem with me?

BRENDAN: Not at all. I think you're very capable.

STEPHANIE: That's not what I meant.

BRENDAN: Look, sweetheart, I didn't ask for us to get lumped together on this—but since we have been, let's just shut the fuck up and get on with it, okay?

STEPHANIE: Right.

On the move through busy corridors, she dumps documents in his arms.

Statements, information on the Iranians, the Embassy, and some bits and pieces I researched last night—

AMIR: She's on the way up!

BRENDAN: What about the video?

STEPHANIE: I've got it. If I'd had time to go through it this morning —

BRENDAN: Waste of time. No one could have got them bail.

STEPHANIE: No?

BRENDAN: A bunch of Muslim fanatics wrecking a building and ranting bloody slogans to Allah. Would you bail them?

AMIR: He's on the way down.

STEPHANIE: Every one of these 'fanatics' has been tortured—

LAWYER: [*bumping into them*] Hey, Brendan, Mecca's that way!

He laughs loudly as he goes off.

BRENDAN: Yeah, right…

STEPHANIE *marches on.*

STEPHANIE: —has been tortured by the regime in Iran or it's happened to a member of their family.

BRENDAN: Yeah, well they have to say that, don't they?

STEPHANIE: What?

BRENDAN: To get into the country.

STEPHANIE: And the holocaust never happened, right?

KAMRAN *is led towards them by a* GUARD.

Hello, Kamran. Are you feeling better?

He stares at her.

[*To the* GUARD] Interview Room Two?

GUARD: Yes, ma'am.

STEPHANIE: [*setting off*] That's my client.

BRENDAN: Bloody hell, you've got an easy one there.

> STEPHANIE *stops at the interview room.*

STEPHANIE: Oh, poor baby, might have to work for his money.
They go into the interview room.

♦ ♦ ♦ ♦ ♦

SCENE THREE

An interview room at the Remand Centre.

HAMID *and* JHILA *wait with* AMIR.

STEPHANIE: I'm sorry about the wait. Brendan O'Sullivan, who'll be in charge of your case—Hamid and Jhila Parsi.

HAMID: How do you do?

> *They shake hands.*

JHILA: Hello.

BRENDAN: Right, shall we get started? Please sit down. Where's the list of charges?

HAMID: Please. We are not terrorist. You must go to Judge again.

BRENDAN: Just a second.

JHILA: We cannot stay here. Shop is closed, in Brisbane.

BRENDAN: Look. I can't do anything until I've gone through this. Sit down.

JHILA: [*in Farsi*] I don't like him.

BRENDAN: [*to* AMIR] What did she say?

AMIR: She says she feels she's in very good hands.

BRENDAN: Speak English please.

AMIR: [*to* JHILA, *in Farsi*] Don't speak Farsi, Mum, he doesn't like it. He's a big lawyer, he's going to get us off!

BRENDAN: Everybody happy? Right. You've been charged with causing damage to international diplomatic property and personnel, and since the whole of Australia has seen it on television about twenty times since yesterday, I assume you're not going to be pleading your innocence?

HAMID: We are very sorry—really—we never meant it.

BRENDAN: So, it's a guilty plea?

HAMID *frowns.*

AMIR: I'll say it in Farsi. [*In Farsi*] In the court, Dad—will you say you're guilty?

HAMID: Sorry, yes, it is true we do damage in building, guilty, yes. But not to people. We do not hit anyone.

BRENDAN: [*looking at* STEPHANIE] Okay. So why did this thing happen yesterday?

HAMID: We don't know. It was just sudden sort of madness.

BRENDAN: What sort of madness?

HAMID *frowns.*

Do I have to tell the Judge you were insane?

HAMID: Insane?

AMIR: [*in Farsi*] Off your head, Dad, crazy!

HAMID: [*in Farsi*] I'm not crazy.

AMIR: [*in Farsi*] But you said 'madness'—that's what it means.

HAMID: [*in Farsi*] Oh shit—no—not madness—I meant anger.

JHILA: [*in Farsi*] They have twenty meanings for every word.

AMIR: [*in English*] He meant 'angry'.

HAMID: We had to protest. Mullah planes kill with bombs fifteen hundred people in Mojahedin... freedom fighters' camp. We have friends there.

BRENDAN: What's 'Mullah'?

AMIR: They rule Iran—sort of mad vicars, with turbans.

BRENDAN: So you came down to Canberra to seek revenge on the government you thought had committed a crime against your friends.

HAMID: No, no, not revenge. Just to make people know. To protest, banners and so on. There were no guards at Embassy. We had paint, some red fizzy drinks, gate is open, my friend run in and we just follow. It was like all bad things that happened in Iran come before my eyes, like movie film.

STEPHANIE: Hang on, Hamid. The gate was open?

HAMID: Yes. One of the Embassy cars left, gate never shut.

JHILA: [*in English*] Everyone has sorrow—torture in prison—

HAMID: We have... out of control, you know, we don't know what happens to us. We are not violent people.

1998 Matrix Theatre Company production at the La Boite Theatre, Brisbane. Above: From left Sandro Colarelli, Joss McWilliam and Caroline Kennison. Below: From left Eugene Gilfedder as Hamid, Angelina Quick as Jhila, Caroling Kennison as Stephanie and Yalin Ozucelik as Amir.
(Photos: Melanie Gray)

BRENDAN: No?

STEPHANIE: So you only went to the Embassy to protest?

HAMID: Yes.

BRENDAN: But it wasn't just a protest was it, Mr Parsi? People got hurt. Are you aware that you are considered to be terrorists?

HAMID: Terrorist—no—they are all thinking we are bunch of bad people, you know? That we bring our problems to this country.

BRENDAN: The Iranian Embassy staff have made further allegations against you this morning—that passports and American dollars were stolen during the raid. Did you steal them?

HAMID: Why would we need passports? They are told to say these things! Iranian Government is terrorist. They do all those hijacks and bombings around world, you know?

BRENDAN: Are you members of the Mojahedin?

HAMID: No.

BRENDAN: Do you have contacts with the Mojahedin?

HAMID: No. But friends, family in their camp. They fight regime.

BRENDAN: So it was just coincidence, was it, that the raid happened at the same time as ten other violent attacks on Iranian embassies all over the world?

HAMID: We did not know that.

BRENDAN: How do you think it looks to ordinary Australians?

HAMID: I don't know.

BRENDAN: It looks like you are part of a global plot, mate.

HAMID: No, no! We heard Mojahedin were killed. We were angry. I say we did not know about other attacks. I say to Judge same thing.

BRENDAN: And he thinks you're a liar!

STEPHANIE: Gentlemen, come on. Hamid, please, sit down. I think we should all just calm down.

JHILA: [*in Farsi*] No one understands.

STEPHANIE: [*to* BRENDAN] It's not the bloody Inquisition.

AMIR: [*in Farsi*] It's all right, Mum.

STEPHANIE: Jhila—Hamid, we know you're not terrorists. Brendan's just asking questions the Prosecution might ask. We're on your side.

HAMID: I understand, it's okay.

JHILA: When can we go home?

BRENDAN: Could be days, could be weeks.

AMIR: But they gave themselves up!

BRENDAN: It's a serious crime—you don't get bail straight away.

JHILA: But we cannot stay here—we have business.

BRENDAN: You should have thought of that before.

HAMID: This is no good. We must have press conference. Tell Australians the truth. Stephanie, you do this?

STEPHANIE: Perhaps it would be best to let things settle for a while?

HAMID: Australians must hear about regime—understand why we did it.

BRENDAN: Australians hear about troubles in the Middle East every day. They don't give a shit.

HAMID: You have very bad opinion of your people.

> BRENDAN *laughs.*

We don't want to cause trouble. We love this country, you know—it is very suitable for Iranians—we have beautiful life here. We are Australian citizen, since four years—

BRENDAN: And when this country let you in you swore an oath to uphold the law.

HAMID: We are law abiding! I ask you for press conference.

BRENDAN: It's not one of your statutory rights.

HAMID: I am your customer, you are my lawyer—

BRENDAN: And as your lawyer, I am telling you the idea is ridiculous.

HAMID: Okay, from now—hunger strike. No food until press conference.

AMIR: Dad!

JHILA: I too.

HAMID: This is free country, I have right to speak.

> *Pause.*

STEPHANIE: Can I just pursue something for a minute?

BRENDAN: Go ahead.

STEPHANIE: Hamid. You say you want the press conference to show you're not terrorists?

HAMID: Exactly.

STEPHANIE: All right. Then to do that you'd have to demonstrate that you are not a threat to Australians.

HAMID: Of course.

STEPHANIE: You'd have to show them that you are peaceful, ordinary people, just like them.

HAMID: Well, I suppose, there are things I could say—

AMIR: What about the Boltons, Dad?

HAMID: I don't know...

STEPHANIE: Who are they?

AMIR: He saved their lives in Tehran. They live on the Gold Coast.

STEPHANIE: They're Australians?

AMIR: Yeah.

STEPHANIE: [*to* HAMID] And you saved their lives in Iran?

> HAMID *nods.*

[*To* BRENDAN] There's your angle!

BRENDAN: Allelujah.

STEPHANIE: Tell us about the Boltons.

BRENDAN: [*going*] I'm out of here.

STEPHANIE: Hang on.

AMIR: Brendan! We weren't just let in, like you said. The Boltons invited us here, sponsored us. Because Dad helped them. See, we're sitting in this park in Tehran, and we hear shouts. And we see this woman...

> *He grabs* STEPHANIE.

... standing in front of some guards—and her husband's over here—

> *He grabs* BRENDAN.

She's screaming 'James, James!'—he's shouting 'Stay there' to their kid. The guards are calling her a whore. I run to Mum and Dad and say 'Something's happening!'

> *The armed* GUARDS *grab* PENNY *and* JAMES BOLTON *(the same actors who play* STEPHANIE *and* BRENDAN*) and corner them.* HAMID *watches.*

PENNY: [*to her unseen son*] Jonathan, wait! [*To the* GUARDS] Please, what have I done? I'm Australian. Visitor.

GUARD ONE: [*in Farsi*] We can see your feet. Filthy western slut.

JAMES: We can't understand you. Speak English!

GUARD TWO: [*in Farsi*] You're lucky we don't slice that shit off your mouth with a razor.

JAMES *puts his hand in front of the barrel of the gun.*

PENNY: James! [*To a* GUARD] Don't shoot! We're Australians! You
can't do this. We have a small son. Please. Look—chador, chador!

GUARD ONE: [*in English, indicating that he can see her exposed foot*]
Foot! Foot! Bad Islam.

AMIR: Dad says 'Don't argue—they kill easy.' Mum says—what did
you say, Mum?

JHILA: I say 'No, Hamid! They might kill you too!'

PENNY: [*to* JAMES] For God's sake, do what he says.

JAMES: All right, all right.

GUARD ONE: You come.

Both Australians are marched off roughly.

PENNY: Run, Jonathan! Run!

AMIR: Dad says to Mum 'Get their kid', and he follows them to one
of those houses where they torture people and they come out after
four hours.

HAMID: They are not tortured, Amir, just questioned.

AMIR: I know—Dad runs to them, he says 'Hey over here! Taxi!'

HAMID: Is not real taxi, just my car.

AMIR: Doesn't matter, Dad—!

HAMID: [*in Farsi*] If you're going to tell it, tell it right.

STEPHANIE: Go on, Amir.

AMIR: Dad brings the Boltons home.

JHILA: They know Hamid risk life to help.

HAMID: I am… wanted by regime.

AMIR: They want to get us out of Tehran. They go back and do all the
official stuff to get us into Australia. So we go to Pakistan.

JHILA: But Singapore first for refugee status.

BRENDAN: [*to* HAMID] They let you leave Iran, when you were wanted?

HAMID: No, no—you got to be kidding. If I leave with them, I get shot.
I find smuggler. I escape!

> AMIR *jumps up onto one of the cages beckoning to all the other
> actors who jump on with him.* AMIR *reaches for his dad, and*
> HAMID *gets on reluctantly. The ute lurches into life. The escapees
> are crushed and jostled as it speeds along. They clap a sharp,
> fast rhythm, reflecting their fear and excitement.*

AMIR: Dad ends up in this ute with thirteen Jews. A hundred miles an hour through a desert town—

HAMID: At this rate we'll get stopped for speeding!

AMIR: And then they hang a left and they're in the middle of nowhere. No lights, no moon, boulders all over the desert and still a hundred miles an hour. Maybe forty times, a guy listens to the ground for cars and waves them on when it's clear. No road, nothing. Heading for Pakistan blind.

The ute stops suddenly.

JEW ONE: Why have we stopped now? What's happened?

DRIVER: We've got to push—out. We're stuck in sand.

They all get out.

AMIR: All the others watch as Dad single-handedly pushes the ute—

HAMID: Amir—we all pushed. Okay?

AMIR: Oh yeah—they all pushed. But Dad's the leader.

JEW ONE: Look! There's a car!

He starts to wave. The DRIVER *grabs him and clamps his arms by his side.*

DRIVER: You want to get us all killed? Only guards use headlights. Come on—for God's sake push it over the border! I've got a lot of money riding on this.

They now start pushing furiously, heaving the cage along, singing rhythmically, 'Ya habib, ya habib', in place of a western shout of, 'Heave, heave'.

HAMID: Come on! It's going!

JEW TWO: Quick!

With a lurch the ute moves over the dune—the cage is upended.

HAMID: Pakistan!

They cheer, but suddenly crouch as the guard car passes, then congratulate each other and climb onto the ute.

DRIVER: Hey—out! You're on foot from here.

HAMID: Which way?

DRIVER: You got twenty dollars?

JEW ONE: We paid already!

DRIVER: That way.

AMIR: They walk through the desert to a village where they sleep.

They all drop to the ground. Pause. The SMUGGLER *comes rushing in.*

SMUGGLER: [*suddenly*] Come on. Time to get up, ladies.

HAMID *and another passenger—played by* AMIR—*sit up drowsily.*

HAMID: What? Where are the others?

SMUGGLER: They've gone. Get these on. It's your wedding day, sweethearts. [*He throws chadors at their feet.*] You've got ten minutes. Make yourselves as pretty as you can.

The MEN *don the chadors, helped by two* WOMEN *who giggle.* AMIR *laughs and tries to make* HAMID *do a belly dance.*

HAMID: Amir! There was none of that—we were too scared.

Wedding music begins, with bells and drums.

SMUGGLER: Okay, you're a wedding party. We've got to get through a guard post. No talking, and keep your faces covered.

The two WOMEN *lead the small procession. They ululate on a high note. At the guard post two* GUARDS *inspect them, stopping suspiciously at* HAMID *and* AMIR. *They point them out to the main* GUARD *who is handed money by the* SMUGGLER. *He waves them on.*

AMIR: It's against the law for a man to lift a woman's veil!

All drop their chadors.

Dad made it to Karachi but it took nine months to get on a plane to Australia. He gave away his last hundred dollars to the friend who'd escaped with him. He said we didn't need it anymore—everything was beautiful where we were going.

PENNY *and* JAMES BOLTON *appear.*

PENNY: Coooee!

JAMES: Welcome to the lucky country, mate!

They hug HAMID *and* JHILA.

AMIR: There were flashbulbs going off all around us.

> JAMES *shakes* HAMID*'s hand.*

JHILA: What is all the cameras?

JAMES: Don't worry about them.

PENNY: [*putting an arm around* JHILA] Everyone's very interested in you. We've got them all on a roster. Only one interview a day.

JHILA: [*in Farsi*] I don't want publicity, Hamid. It's dangerous.

JAMES: [*sensing her fear*] Cheer up, love. You're in Australia now. No worries. Come and get your first Aussie beer!

> *He moves them along.*

AMIR: And Dad said—

HAMID: This is happiest day of my life!

> *He is brought up short, confronted with* KAMRAN *who is sitting alone.*

AMIR: [*to* BRENDAN *and* STEPHANIE] A whole bunch of people welcomed us as well as newspapers and TV cameras. He handled them then, he can handle them now. He can tell them all this.

> HAMID *unfolds a piece of paper.*

STEPHANIE: [*to* BRENDAN] If he just sticks to that, with the take-away shop, the barbecues, the beers—we're laughing.

BRENDAN: If he sticks to the story—all right. Do what you like.

♦ ♦ ♦ ♦ ♦

SCENE FOUR

Press Conference at the Remand Centre the next day.

Two JOURNALISTS *move around* HAMID *like sharks.* JOURNALIST ONE *shines a hand-held light in* HAMID*'s face.* BRENDAN, STEPHANIE, JHILA *and* KAMRAN *are nearby.* AMIR *is apart.*

HAMID: [*reading a statement*] In the name of God, in the name of oppressed but brave people of Iran, and in the name of all who fight for freedom. Ladies and gentlemen. Professor Rajavi, brother of leader of Mojahedin, said 'History of human rights in Iran is being written by our bloods'. Sirs, he was right. Embassy protest was reaction to bombing of our friends and families by Iranian F4 fighter bombers. And now, myself and these ten others, we also are bombed by media accusing us as terrorists. If you will forgive, you get wrong guys! [*He laughs.*] Why does Trading Minister apologise to regime condemned by Amnesty International, regime that is supporter of state terrorism, regime that insists on assassinating Mr Rushdie?

> JOURNALIST TWO *takes the light from* JOURNALIST ONE.

Dear journalists, we all are here, as political refugee, because basic human rights violated. So today, we are bringing judgement to Australian people. To try us in own court of conscious. Put your feet in our steps, for only one minute. Try to feel our pain. Kamran—he was professor, at university. On his feet, there are no toes—

> JOURNALIST TWO *stops moving.*

—cut by electric scissor, and scars from boiling water many times.

> JOURNALIST TWO *shines the light on* KAMRAN *briefly.*

Broken bones. Fingers cut. Worse things also. He is man of dignity, but I must tell… he would forgive if he hears me… they… they also put a… cut bottle… glass in his… back… in his behind, gentlemen… and… I'm sorry…

JOURNALIST ONE: [*grabbing the light*] We understand that you're not taking solid food. Is this—?

STEPHANIE: Would you all please give Mr Parsi a moment!

HAMID: Hunger strike is because terrorists can speak their side in papers, but we are locked in and no equal chance to speak. We are very… suspicious people, I think, of system here.

JOURNALIST ONE: In what way, suspicious?

HAMID: We worry that we are make to look as terrorist.

JOURNALIST TWO: [*grabbing the light, moving around*] So you're saying you think you're being set up?

STEPHANIE: Don't answer that, Hamid.

HAMID: It's okay, I handle. All we say is, about hunger strike, if they will let us be more talking with you people we will eat. Or all starved bodies will go out one after one.

JOURNALIST ONE: [*grabbing the light, changing direction*] Do you think Australians understand the political point you're trying to make?

HAMID: Unfortunately, Australians… politically are very… naïve—

　　JOURNALIST TWO takes the light.

—and… I'm sorry, forgive me for my phrase, very ignorant of international politics. In western world, as you know, a lot of court judgements affected by media. This is—I am not trying to—tell you what your job is, but in reality—this is duty of you gentlemen, to inform public.

　　They all laugh loudly.

JOURNALIST TWO: Thank you for reminding us.

　　Laughter.

So you don't accept that you should be subject to Australian law?

HAMID: Yes to law, but a fair, fair judgement—from jury people—

JOURNALIST TWO: And will you accept the verdict that the jury gives you?

HAMID: You think we have any choices here?

　　He laughs dryly. The JOURNALISTS *now both move in the same direction.*

JOURNALIST TWO: Do you accept that you look fanatical on the TV footage?

HAMID: No, no, that sort of thing, fanatics, is back in Iran. Please—

JOURNALIST ONE: [*taking the light, speeding up the circling*] How do you explain the violence?

HAMID: Well, I don't consider it violent—

JOURNALIST TWO: An official sustained a serious head injury.

HAMID: It was not serious. Why you—?

JOURNALIST TWO: That wasn't violent?

HAMID: No. Why you question like this? Look at Kamran. Tortured and what is done to mind—and again family bombed, and then you say 'is he fanatic and violence?' I say no, he is normal man.

JOURNALIST ONE: [*taking the light, standing still*] So why didn't he kill someone?

HAMID: What?

JOURNALIST ONE: What stopped any of you killing someone?

> KAMRAN *lunges at* HAMID, *who grabs his arms.*

JHILA: [*screaming*] Kamran!

> *General commotion.*

HAMID: It's all right.

BRENDAN: Okay, that's it folks. We'll wind it up there.

STEPHANIE: [*tending to* KAMRAN] Could we have some help here please?

HAMID: It's all right.

> KAMRAN *is escorted away.*

JHILA: [*in Farsi*] Why did he do that?

HAMID: [*in Farsi*] I don't know.

AMIR: Why didn't you tell the story, Dad?

HAMID: [*in Farsi*] I can't talk about barbecues and beers, and forget the people who are suffering there now. You remember that!

JHILA: [*in English*] Like jackals kill buffalo. In pack. When buffalo falls, they get it.

GUARD: This way please.

> *He takes them away.*

BRENDAN: Better tell Mummy and Daddy not to watch the midday news.

STEPHANIE: Fuck off. What the hell was he doing?

BRENDAN: I thought he did all right.

STEPHANIE: [*on the move*] If he'd done what I'd said, we'd have bail tomorrow.

BRENDAN: I blame the white overalls—made them look darker than ever.

♦ ♦ ♦ ♦ ♦

SCENE FIVE

The Remand Centre. A cell.

STEPHANIE: I thought you wanted us to help you clear your names?

HAMID: No! Wanted to be clear why we protest. And they hear me!

STEPHANIE: Yes! And you sounded like a terrorist.

HAMID: Terrorist? No!

STEPHANIE: People pick up on key words—they hear 'hunger strike', they hear 'Mojahedin'—

HAMID: They say words to me like... fanatic—

STEPHANIE: If you go on like this to the press, or in court, you'll go to jail.

> HAMID *shakes his head.*

We must start working together, Hamid.

AMIR: Dad just said those things because he wanted to help people who are still back in Iran.

BRENDAN: It doesn't matter why he said it.

AMIR: It does! How can people find him innocent if they don't know why he went to the Embassy? Dad just started in the middle, that's all. [*To* HAMID] Tell them about Masud.

HAMID: [*in Farsi*] That's not important.

STEPHANIE: Who's this?

AMIR: Dad's friend. That's when it all started and he ended up being tortured. Tell them, Dad.

HAMID: [*in English*] I say too much already today.

STEPHANIE: Not about yourself.

JHILA: [*in Farsi*] You don't have to.

BRENDAN: Speaking the same language would be a start.

JHILA: [*in Farsi, at* BRENDAN] There's no point telling the deaf.

AMIR: [*in Farsi*] Mum! [*He turns to* HAMID.] How can they fix things up if they don't know?

HAMID: [*in Farsi*] Amir, leave it!

AMIR: [*in Farsi*] You talked to the press, why not your own lawyers?

HAMID: [*in Farsi*] Quiet!

> BRENDAN *looks at his watch.*

AMIR: [*in Farsi*] God, Dad, you're stupid!

JHILA: [*in Farsi*] Show some respect!

BRENDAN: Bloody Arabs.

JHILA: [*in English*] What you say?

BRENDAN: I said it's a pity we don't speak Arab.

STEPHANIE: Arabic.

JHILA: [*in English*] We are Iranian. Is Farsi.
BRENDAN: [*muttering to* STEPHANIE] Same difference.

◆ ◆ ◆ ◆ ◆

SCENE SIX

Amir's family home, Tehran, Iran. 1982.

AMIR: There's this joke in Iran—'What's the difference between an Iranian and an Arab? The Arab lives for sex and making money, the Iranian lives for sex and making money—and culture.' Does nothing for me. But it's very popular with Tehran taxi drivers. The first time I heard it I was three, in a taxi, going to see Dad in prison with Mum and Granddad.

JHILA *lovingly examines the carpet in their room.*

Mum and Dad have this habit of getting themselves into trouble. A lot of Iranians do, especially in Iran. I think it's to do with their in-built love of life being slightly at odds with their Government's belief that this is a world in which we ought not to live. You endure this life and have fun in the next. Only most people can't wait that long.

Faint music. The family dances in the shadows.

It's winter 1982. We live in this big, old house in Tehran, Granddad's house, and we have lots of parties. This one's no different from all the others, only we don't know that this is the day our lives will change forever.

The music gets louder. Lights reveal the family dancing with energy, clapping, drinking. HAMID *is trying to speak to his* FATHER *over the noise, until his* FATHER *breaks away angrily.*

FATHER: My ungrateful son! My first born! You've killed your father… I'll never see you again.
HAMID: It's an hour's drive away, Dad. We'll see you on weekends.
REZA: Talk business tomorrow!
JHILA: No, Reza, we want this settled now.
REZA: We're trying to have a good time!
JHILA: It's all right for you, you and Neda got out of here!

AMIR: All the sons and their wives live upstairs—with Granddad downstairs. The basement has no windows, so it's the centre for forbidden activities. A public flogging is the minimum penalty for enjoying yourself, but if booze is banned you want to drink more, and if music is banned you want to play it more.

A burst of music as the FATHER's *eldest daughter* NEDA *dances wildly. The boys clap.*

FATHER: I offer you my world, and you throw it in my face. Neda, stop making a fool of yourself. Look, I'm crying! All for this stupid job—

HAMID: Please, Dad—

JHILA: It's a good job, head of the department.

FATHER: What's wrong with working for your father? Liaising with clients.

HAMID: Rent collecting is fine. But I need a regular income for Amir.

FATHER: So you leave me all alone, your poor father.

JHILA: Alone? You have three other sons, two daughters, and four wives.

AMIR: Four wives is weird, even in Iran.

NEDA: Look what you've done to him. Why don't you just go? I'll comfort your father and my Reza will be proud to collect the rents.

FATHER: Shut up, woman! Reza's an idiot. I want Hamid by my side.

HAMID: I know, Dad, I know…

JHILA: Can't you see what he's doing?

HAMID: Ssh!

FATHER: But of course you have to make up your own mind.

HAMID: Dad… I… oh, I don't know what to do for the best.

FATHER: You go, son, you and little Jhila, you go. Go and do your Health and Safety… whatever…

HAMID: Maybe I could commute?

JHILA: Hamid, we decided! No.

FATHER: I've taught him to be a man—now I pay the price.

JHILA: Oh yes! Taught him to be a man—so that he can lock up your tenants' toilets until they pay!

HAMID: After a week of holding their shit, they pay up—money that allows you to live under his roof and eat his food!

JHILA: And we agreed that we wouldn't do that anymore!

FATHER: I'll die soon anyway…

HAMID: No, Dad!

JHILA: Oh, God!

FATHER: Nothing for you to worry about.

HAMID: It's not that I want to go, Dad…

FATHER: Leave me, leave me!

HAMID: All right.

JHILA: Hamid?

HAMID: I'll stay.

FATHER: Oh, my son!

> *He embraces* HAMID.

JHILA: That's it.

> *She moves away.*

HAMID: So… when do you want me to start work?

FATHER: Soon, soon. The man I've got now is good. We just can't throw him out.

HAMID: You've already got someone?

FATHER: It won't be long. Come on, let's not talk about that now. Let's drink! I'm a happy man! [*He dances away from them.*] I'm a happy man.

HAMID: [*going to* JHILA] I couldn't hurt him, all right? He's an old man!

JHILA: He's a wily, old man. Look at him now that he's got his own way.

HAMID: That's enough.

JHILA: We had an agreement!

HAMID: Keep your voice down.

JHILA: What's the point? We live in a glass house—if they don't hear us, they read our lips! You said you wanted the same things as me—our own place, peace and quiet—but he starts crying and it all means nothing.

HAMID: Jhila.

JHILA: I'm getting out of this prison.

> *She goes to their room.*

HAMID: You don't know what you're doing.
JHILA: Shoes, shoes!

>*He takes them off.*

You can see Amir whenever you like.
HAMID: If you walk out of here, that's it, goodbye. And watch me, I'll have four wives!
AMIR: Mum, Dad—don't shout.
JHILA: Shhsh, don't cry.

>*She comforts the three-year-old* AMIR.

HAMID: See what you've done!

>*There's a knock on the door, then silence.*

Hello? [*Pause.*] Hello?
JHILA: [*whispering*] You answer it, I'll go and warn them.

>*She takes* AMIR *and hurries to the stairs.*

HAMID: Jhila! Take this…

>*He hands her his glass and she goes.*

>♦ ♦ ♦ ♦ ♦

SCENE SEVEN

The same.

MASUD: [*offstage*] Hello?
HAMID: I'm coming.
MASUD: [*offstage*] Open up.
HAMID: Who is it?
MASUD: [*offstage, with a low chuckle*] Surprise.

>MASUD *appears.*

Hello.
HAMID: Masud.

>*They look at one another, then smile, laugh and embrace.*

Masud! I don't believe it!
MASUD: Well, I'd be amazed too, only I knew I was coming.
HAMID: I thought it was the guards!

MASUD: You been doing something you shouldn't?

HAMID: Depends on whose side you're on! Come in!

> MASUD *sees the carpet.*

MASUD: [*touching it*] Jhila's carpet.

HAMID: Where've you been? Three years away and not a word. We thought you'd died.

MASUD: [*taking off his shoes*] Not yet.

> *Pause.*

HAMID: It's so good to see you.

MASUD: And you. How's Jhila?

HAMID: She's fine. She's downstairs… with our son.

MASUD: A son? [*Pause.*] Congratulations.

> *They shake hands.*

HAMID: Thank you.

> MASUD *looks out the window. A* GUARD *walks past.*

HAMID: You okay?

MASUD: Hmm? Yeah. Look, Hamid, I need your help.

HAMID: Of course. Anything.

MASUD: I need to keep out of sight for a few days.

HAMID: Stay here.

MASUD: I got into a bit of trouble… It's a long story—

> JHILA *enters and gasps. She puts down the imaginary* AMIR.

Hello, beautiful.

JHILA: Masud!

> *They embrace.*

I thought I'd never see you again.

MASUD: You haven't changed a bit.

JHILA: Where've you been?

MASUD: All over the place. [*To* AMIR] And who's this?

AMIR: I'm Amir.

MASUD: Amir. I like that name. How old are you?

JHILA: Two.

AMIR: [*overlapping*] I'm nearly three.

JHILA: He's two.

AMIR *fetches a musical box and holds it out.*

MASUD: What's this? [*He takes it and opens the lid.*] Listen.

The music plays.

JHILA: I don't let him touch it.

MASUD: Careful. Let her dance or she'll break.

They all listen to the music until JHILA *suddenly shuts the lid. The tune stops and she takes the box.*

Look at us! Like we're strangers.

JHILA: Wait a minute.

She puts the *musical box away and helps* AMIR *to bed.*

MASUD: He's a lovely boy.

HAMID: Yeah…

JHILA: [*to* AMIR] Good night.

She searches for something.

MASUD: [*checking out the window*] All the family still here?

HAMID: Yeah—come and say hello.

MASUD: If you don't mind, I'm tired.

HAMID: Of course. [*To* JHILA] Masud's staying.

MASUD: Is that all right?

JHILA: You're welcome. [*Producing vodka*] It came at a very high price—I had to be nice to your father to get it.

MASUD: Don't you know it's against the law?

HAMID: What? Well yes, but—

HAMID *and* JHILA *exchange looks.* MASUD *chuckles.*

Give me that!

HAMID *pours three drinks.*

MASUD: No—not for me.

HAMID: What?

MASUD: I don't drink anymore.

HAMID: Now I know you're joking!

MASUD: No, really—but you go ahead.

JHILA: You don't drink? You?

MASUD: It—doesn't agree with me.

HAMID: But… oh well… your health!

They drink.

Come on—

A knock. MASUD *jumps.*

FATHER: Is everything all right, Hamid?
HAMID: Fine, Dad, fine. Good night.
FATHER: Good night.

Pause.

JHILA: Why have you come back, Masud?
MASUD: I haven't been away. I've been working here.
JHILA: And you didn't tell us?

Pause.

HAMID: Masud's in a bit of trouble.
JHILA: What have you done?
HAMID: Maybe he doesn't want to talk about it.
JHILA: [*at speed*] Shut up, Hamid. He can tell us if he wants to.
HAMID: It's none of our business—
JHILA: Was it the black market?
MASUD: No…
JHILA: A woman?
HAMID: Jhila! Masud. Have a drink.

MASUD *declines. Pause.*

JHILA: Drugs?
HAMID: Shut up!
MASUD: Hamid.
HAMID: Really, Masud—I mean it—you just relax.

MASUD *sees* AMIR.

MASUD: Hey, what are you doing awake?
JHILA: [*to* HAMID, *whispering*] What's going on?
HAMID: [*whispering, irritated*] I don't know, shh!
MASUD: Well, well—

He picks little AMIR *up, holds him high, running around the room. The adult* AMIR *laughs.*

Here we go, here we go! We're bombing the nasty, old Ayatollah's house—bang, bang, bang! Got him. Let's land on Daddy—wheee…

AMIR: Help, help!

JHILA: You two! Come on—that's enough.

She grabs little AMIR *and replaces him on his bed.*

Sleep.

AMIR: No.

JHILA: [*to* AMIR] Show Masud how good you are. Off to sleep, now.

MASUD: [*singing*] 'Let's go down to the tavern, my friend—'

JHILA: Sshh!

MASUD: [*singing, a little quieter*] '—seeking girls and booze and song…'

JHILA: Masud!

HAMID *laughs.*

MASUD: [*singing, like a lullaby*] 'With a glass in one hand, and a girl in the other, we'll drink, we'll drink, we'll drink and then we'll have them, then we'll have them all the night long!' [*Pause.*] I only know two songs.

He hums to little AMIR.

HAMID: Last time I heard you sing that, you were pissed out of your brain, standing on a table in the Palace Night Club.

MASUD: [*joining them on the carpet*] You'd just told me you were getting married. The revolution was nearly over.

JHILA: We were putting roses in the soldiers' guns.

HAMID: A beautiful time.

MASUD: Our victory. We thought we'd got everything we wanted. And then the Shah cried—television tears. I laughed so much I thought I'd have a heart attack.

HAMID *laughs.*

JHILA: I cried. When the Shah cried. He called our country a beautiful, crystal vase—and it was broken. We broke it, he said. Smashed and ugly and never to be mended.

MASUD: It was easy to break. It was cracked, collecting dust, full of rotting flowers.

JHILA: We were free. I loved my Levis—you used to whistle at me in a mini-skirt—you danced on a table in a night club!

MASUD: Sure, but I couldn't write what I wanted.

JHILA: At least people could be themselves.

MASUD: Strutting down the street in Dior suits and fur coats? Driving fast, imported cars? Was that Iranian? What about the beggars living in the rubbish dump?

JHILA: I was happier. I'd go back.

HAMID: You've just forgotten.

JHILA: Look what's happened since the revolution. My mother always said never trust a Mullah.

MASUD: True. We were responsible for letting Khomeini in. We couldn't see him for what he was.

JHILA: I saw him clearly. The minute he stepped off the plane from his exile. He said he felt nothing about being back here in his own country. I hated him while you all cheered.

HAMID: Yes, yes, Jhila, you were cleverer than all of us.

Pause.

MASUD: So the fight goes on.

HAMID: A few fight. The rest of us just keep quiet.

JHILA: We have no choice.

MASUD: In silence lies obedience.

JHILA: What do you mean?

MASUD: If you want a civilized, democratic society you can't just sit around, you have to fight for it.

JHILA: Like the Mojahedin, who kill for democracy?

MASUD: It's the only thing this regime understands.

JHILA: I can't believe I'm hearing this from you.

MASUD: Well, if you like being forced to wear a chador, having no freedom of speech, public floggings—

JHILA: No one likes it, but I wouldn't kill to change it.

MASUD: Then they'll go on killing hundreds of people each day in the jails, on the streets. And not just in this country—

HAMID: It's true.

MASUD: What if they took Amir—would you kill to save him?

JHILA: That's different—what a mother feels.

MASUD: The principle's the same. You fight the thing which threatens your child, or it will kill your child.

JHILA: You used to be a pacifist.

Pause.

MASUD: You remember my sister, Maryam?

HAMID: Beautiful girl.

MASUD: [*unsentimental*] Well, two years ago she went shopping with her neighbour, Pargal. A guard stopped them because Maryam's chador had slipped back from her forehead. He could just see a wisp of black hair. She couldn't cover it with her arms full so the guard arrested her. And Pargal for her big mouth. There were a hundred women maybe, old, young, pregnant, all driven in buses to the prison, and then one of the guards told them they'd be fined. Pargal accused them of arresting them only to get rich. So the Mullah in charge ordered eighty lashes for all of them. They took them one at a time to a cell, and they were handcuffed face down and lashed. It came to Pargal's turn. And they're just going to hit her when she says, 'Maryam Amini has a brother in the Mojahedin'. They released her. Maryam was tortured for seven hours. She kept silent. So they condemned her to death. At seventeen. They can't execute virgins, so the guards in the firing squad wrote down their names for a lottery and the winner conducted the rape. A Mullah signed Maryam's marriage certificate after she was dead. It came in the mail to our parents' house. With a box of chocolates. That's when I knew that to do nothing is to allow them to do anything.

HAMID: That's all it takes? One woman's word for them to kill her?

MASUD: They need two witnesses. Her husband backed her up.

HAMID: But to lie—and kill an innocent girl.

JHILA: It wasn't a lie.

MASUD: No.

HAMID: What?

MASUD: I'm with the Mojahedin.

Pause.

HAMID: You?

MASUD: I'm sorry I couldn't tell you earlier. I had to be sure—

HAMID: You didn't trust us?

MASUD *shrugs.*

JHILA: And now you're sure you can?

HAMID: Jhila!

MASUD: This is the last safe place I know.

HAMID: Yes. You're safe with us.

JHILA: What do you do then—write for their news sheet?

MASUD: At first I did.

JHILA: And now—

HAMID: He kills Mullahs! What do you think he does—make the tea?

MASUD: I was doing a job—we were going to get rid of someone—

JHILA: Oh, my God.

MASUD: I have to get out of the country.

JHILA: Did they see you come here?

MASUD: I don't think so.

HAMID: You stay as long as you like.

MASUD: Harbouring a member of the Mojahedin can carry a death sentence.

HAMID: What would they want with me? If they find out you're here I'll say you're my old university friend just visiting, no problem.

MASUD: It's not as simple as that.

HAMID: Masud. You don't understand. For a friend we'll do anything.

JHILA: You must stay.

> *Pause.*

MASUD: I'm grateful to you both.

> JHILA *lights a candle by the mirror, then starts to make beds.*

I won't be here long—I've just got to find a smuggler to get me to Paris. Then I can work again. With the National Council of Resistance.

HAMID: We can ask Reza, my sister's husband, he knows people who have dealings with them. You're safe here—

MASUD: Thank you.

HAMID: You in the Mojahedin.

MASUD: [*laughing*] Yeah—the perennial coward.

HAMID: What do they do to you, if they catch you?

MASUD: If we have a chance, we take cyanide.

HAMID: In a… like a… capsule?

MASUD *nods.*

You'll swallow poison, but not vodka?

They smile.

I'm sorry about Jhila earlier—women don't understand.

JHILA *overhears.*

MASUD: It's good that she says what she thinks. A lot of our people are women.

HAMID: They are? My God.

JHILA: [*sharply*] Commanders.

MASUD: [*smiling*] Yes.

JHILA: I've heard about them. At university.

She finishes the beds.

HAMID: [*in a low voice*] But Jhila's not like them. I'd be with you if I could. You know that, don't you?

MASUD *slumps.*

Come on.

He helps him to the bed.

MASUD: I haven't slept for three days— [*To* JHILA] Thank you for this bed.

JHILA: [*smiling*] I'm glad you're here.

MASUD: So am I.

He kisses her, then produces a rose from his bag.

For you… It's from your garden.

She smiles. HAMID *goes to bed.* JHILA *places the rose in front of the mirror and lies down beside* HAMID.

[*Singing, lying down*] 'From morning to dusk, I whisper to my heart the story of your injustice, but before the story unwinds—you are the one it wants, you are the one it wants'… That's the other one.

HAMID *laughs.* MASUD *sleeps.*

JHILA: [*whispering*] What have we done?

HAMID: He's got nowhere else to go.

◆ ◆ ◆ ◆ ◆

SCENE EIGHT

The Remand Centre.

STEPHANIE *is in a guarded cell with* KAMRAN, *who speaks English.*

STEPHANIE: Please, Kamran, try to answer. [*Pause.*] All right. Do you remember when you went inside the Embassy? Nothing?

    Pause.

KAMRAN: My heart my head my foot my stomach my lower.
STEPHANIE: Yes?
KAMRAN: It bothering me.
STEPHANIE: The doctor will come.
KAMRAN: I supposed visit my doctor today. I can make charges against you. You are holding me here.
STEPHANIE: It won't be for long.

    BRENDAN *pokes his head in.*

Kamran, can you tell me about the Embassy? The rose garden?

    She sighs.

BRENDAN: It's five forty-five. I'm off.
STEPHANIE: Hang on—we're supposed to be looking at the video again.
BRENDAN: Is that necessary?
STEPHANIE: Yes. But it'll have to be at my place. I'm babysitting.
BRENDAN: All right. You still in the same flat?
STEPHANIE: Yes.
BRENDAN: Seven-thirty?
STEPHANIE: Whenever.
BRENDAN: Don't get stuck here talking, eh?

    He leaves.

STEPHANIE: [*to the* GUARD] I'd love to know what's going on inside his head.
GUARD: No one home.

◆ ◆ ◆ ◆ ◆

SCENE NINE

Hamid and Jhila's room.

All sleep, except AMIR.

AMIR: My eyes are wide open, but I keep quiet. I can see Masud on the floor. My mother has put a mirror near the candle—the mirror she keeps for New Year—and I see a burnt-out insect float down the glass. Masud stirs. I want to tell him he's safe with the mirror there, the mirror to reflect away bad things. He makes strange noises as he sleeps, like our dog on cold, winter nights. I want to go and stroke him. That's what you have to do for the dog. One day, I'll touch him, in this time of Masud as I call it, and he'll wake up and look at me, and he won't be angry, he'll smile. He smells sour, so I hold my breath and watch his eyelids dance. I like him, this Masud. I like him for letting me open the musical box. My mother smiled. Usually she frowns if I touch the ballerina. Now Masud's face is glowing white and I see a dark space grow where his mouth should be, and out of the space comes a sound. And as the sound fills my ears, I know that all the magic mirrors in Iran can't keep us safe.

HAMID: Masud. It's okay.

MASUD: Where's my bag? I've got to leave—

AMIR: Dad!

JHILA: What's going on?

HAMID: It's all right—

AMIR: Dad!

HAMID: Look after Amir.

MASUD: My bag—

HAMID: Masud—you're dreaming. Calm down.

> JHILA *mimes carrying the child. The adult* AMIR *walks with her and puts his arm around her.*

MASUD: Shit. I'm sorry. Did I wake the boy?

HAMID: It's okay.

JHILA: I'll take him into the hall if you're going to talk.

> JHILA *rocks the child slowly.*

MASUD: There's something I should have told you. [*He reaches for his bag and pulls out a gun.*] When I leave here I'm going to have to ask you to get rid of these. You'd have to be careful. There are grenades too. Could you do it?

HAMID: I won't let you down.

JHILA: [*whispering*] If I were Masud, I wouldn't do this to my friends.

MASUD: Hamid. If they come, I'll use them.

HAMID: No problem.

MASUD: You're a good man.

JHILA: If I were Masud, I would not do this to my friends.

SCENE TEN

Stephanie's flat, night.

An actor puts a rose into a plastic tube and gives it to BRENDAN.

STEPHANIE: [*not looking up from her documents*] Door's open.

> BRENDAN *enters with a bottle of Shiraz and the rose, which* STEPHANIE *takes.*

How very appropriate.

BRENDAN: A peace offering.

STEPHANIE: Yes, well…

> *She discards it carelessly.*

BRENDAN: Where's this baby, then?

STEPHANIE: Never mind the baby. Let's get on. I've got a few problems with the diplomats' role in all this. Now, the Iranian Embassy rang the police—Brendan?

BRENDAN: That used to be over there.

STEPHANIE: Could you listen, please? The Iranian Embassy rang the police to ask for protection as soon as they heard about the massacre at the Mojahedin camp, okay? It was 2 a.m. on the day of the protest. The staff were expecting trouble. And yet, Hamid says, as the protesters were gathering in the street, they actually opened the gate for a car to leave.

BRENDAN: So what?

STEPHANIE: If there's a prowler outside my house, do I open the door?

BRENDAN: I don't know. Do you?

STEPHANIE: Hamid said they only got inside the building because the diplomat opened the main door.

BRENDAN: What are you saying—they invited them in to beat them up and wreck the place?

STEPHANIE: There's a lot more going on here than meets the eye.

BRENDAN: You wish there was.

STEPHANIE: Well, how do you explain the diplomats waiting a whole day before reporting their safe had been robbed?

BRENDAN: Don't know.

STEPHANIE: Brendan! Sixty-five thousand US dollars, two hundred blank passports? They've made it up!

BRENDAN: So they made it up. It's got nothing to do with the case.

STEPHANIE: I've already run this past Peter, if it comes out in court—

BRENDAN: You won't get them into court. Even if you have evidence they'll claim immunity.

STEPHANIE: They've been baying for blood ever since the raid— they've got the video to back them up.

BRENDAN: Stephanie, we're not going to bring into question the diplomats' role in this. End of story.

STEPHANIE: Even if they incited the whole thing?

BRENDAN: They're not on trial here.

STEPHANIE: All right Brendan, it's obviously too much like hard work—let's just lie on the floor with our legs in the air and submit, shall we?

He smiles.

Oh, piss off.

BRENDAN: What?

STEPHANIE: There's a lot of problems to solve on this case—

BRENDAN: You with your legs in the air would solve a lot of mine.

STEPHANIE: Oh, get out!

BRENDAN: Sorry.

STEPHANIE: You're pathetic.

BRENDAN: Don't kick me out.

STEPHANIE: You want to stay, you work. You want to piss about, fuck off!

BRENDAN: All right, I'll stay.

STEPHANIE: Does that include staying on the case?

BRENDAN: For now. But we'll have a drink first.

STEPHANIE: No.

BRENDAN: Still make you go weak at the knees then?

STEPHANIE: No. I can hold my drink now. I started practising the night you walked out on me.

BRENDAN: [*without pausing*] All right. [*He grabs the remote control.*] This is the way it's going to be. We plead guilty to Hamid damaging the car, to Jhila throwing the bottle at the picture of the Ayatollah, not guilty to injury—he's raising a spanner, but you never see it come down on anyone. Suspended sentences. Cut and dried. They can go back to the shop and we can have a drink.

STEPHANIE: That's your final decision, is it?

BRENDAN: Yep.

STEPHANIE: You don't give a shit about these people, do you?

BRENDAN: They've been involved in a terrorist incident. Let's just say there's no common ground.

    AMIR *listens at the door.*

STEPHANIE: They're opposed to terrorism! That's why they were allowed into Australia in the first place. Don't you see the irony? We recognised Iran's cruelty when we took them in as refugees, but now we turn a blind eye to the regime and happily take its money for sheep or wheat or whatever they want from us!

BRENDAN: You're not in front of the Judge now, Stef.

STEPHANIE: I'm aware of that, Brendan, thanks. It's just that, unlike you, I care that the diplomats don't come out smelling like roses at Hamid and Jhila's expense.

BRENDAN: Horse shit! All you care about is getting your face on television—all this caring, sharing crap—

STEPHANIE: You've always been terrified of anyone with a conscience—

BRENDAN: You're drumming this whole thing up to get yourself a bloody partnership—

STEPHANIE: —because you can't find it in yourself to care about anything except the welfare of your own dick.

BRENDAN *laughs. A knock on the door.*

That'll be the baby.

She moves towards the door.

BRENDAN: What?

AMIR: [*entering*] Hi.

BRENDAN: What's he doing here?

STEPHANIE: He's staying 'til we get bail. Good film?

AMIR: Yeah. [*Pause.*] Hey! [*Picking up the bottle*] Shiraz! That's in Iran.

STEPHANIE: Oh, come on—let's open it.

BRENDAN: You sure, Stef?

She takes the wine, moving away. Silence.

What's Shiraz like?

AMIR: Haven't you had it before?

BRENDAN: The place.

AMIR: Never been there.

Pause. STEPHANIE *eavesdrops.*

BRENDAN: So, do you miss home?

AMIR: Not really.

BRENDAN: You remember it then?

AMIR: I've only been away two days.

BRENDAN: I meant Tehran.

AMIR: Oh. Are you and Stephanie working? Or are you just trying to crack on to her?

BRENDAN: [*after a slight pause*] Been there, done that.

AMIR: She really likes you.

BRENDAN: You reckon?

AMIR: Yeah. Dad says the nastier they are the more they like you. But you shouldn't argue with her. You should just take it. I was getting shit from this girl at school—I'm going out with her now. She's Irish, she can get really angry.

BRENDAN: Right. How old are you?

AMIR: Fourteen. You're Irish, aren't you? O'Sullivan?

BRENDAN: Yeah, way back. Russian too.

STEPHANIE *brings wine and glasses.*

STEPHANIE: Not Russian. Brendan's great-grandmother was Armenian.

AMIR: Hey—you're one of us! Armenia was part of Persia once.

STEPHANIE *laughs loudly at* BRENDAN.

That's what Iran used to be called.

BRENDAN: Yeah, well, it's mainly Irish anyway.

STEPHANIE *hands* AMIR *some wine.*

AMIR: Dad doesn't let me drink.

STEPHANIE: Oh sorry, of course.

BRENDAN: They're Muslims.

AMIR: No. I'm too young.

STEPHANIE: You're not a religious family?

AMIR: No way.

STEPHANIE *laughs lightly at* BRENDAN.

I'm going to bed. Good night. See you, Brendan.

He smiles significantly at BRENDAN.

STEPHANIE: Brendan's leaving the case soon, Amir, so maybe not.

AMIR: What?

BRENDAN: I've got a lot on.

AMIR: But I've told Mum and Dad you're going to get them off!

STEPHANIE: There are lots of famous people getting divorced at the moment.

AMIR: You can't just—

BRENDAN: Sorry, mate.

AMIR: I don't believe this!

He exits.

STEPHANIE: Feel like a piece of shit?

BRENDAN: Do you?

STEPHANIE: You know what your problem is?

BRENDAN: What's yours? That was emotional blackmail.

STEPHANIE: You've lost it. You've forgotten how to take risks.

BRENDAN: You must be bloody desperate, Stef.

◆ ◆ ◆ ◆ ◆

SCENE ELEVEN

Hamid and Jhila's room. Iran. 1982.

AMIR: It's the day of Masud's arrest. The day everything will change. He hasn't been out of the room for two months. Dad has to empty a bucket for him. Mum and I are staying at Grandma's to keep out of the way and when we visit he's always sad. He never plays the musical box anymore. But this is his last day—and he's different.

> MASUD *plays the part of a gorilla for* AMIR *and* JHILA. *He lunges at them wildly, roaring.*

JHILA: [*laughing*] Stop it! Stop! Shhsh!

> *The gorilla stops, then threatens to lunge again.*

No… get away—

MASUD: [*in a gorilla voice*] But there's no one else in the house and I'm coming to get you!

> *He lunges at* JHILA.

AMIR: Get me! Get me!

> MASUD *chases the imaginary* AMIR. *They end up on the floor.*

JHILA: Okay, that's enough children. [*To* AMIR] You're tired. Bed!

MASUD: It's nice to see you smile.

JHILA: [*to* AMIR] Try to sleep.

> *She lays the child down.*

MASUD: My last day, and Reza's got them all to go out on a picnic. [*He sits on the carpet.*] I could have done with the break before this. Come and sit down.

JHILA: I'm too nervous.

MASUD: Of me? No!

JHILA: No.

MASUD: Come on.

> *She sits next to him. He smiles at her.*

JHILA: [*smiling*] Stop it.

MASUD: Just thinking.

JHILA: About what?

MASUD: You might be embarrassed.

JHILA: Oh.

MASUD: You wouldn't want me to say it.

JHILA: I don't mind. [*Pause.*] Tell me.

> *Pause.*

MASUD: My bucket needs emptying.

> *She hits him. They laugh.*

JHILA: [*her laughter turning to tears*] I'm sorry.

MASUD: Jhila. What's the matter?

JHILA: Can't speak.

MASUD: Come on.

> *He comforts her.*

It's all right. It doesn't matter. My life is nothing to me. [*Pause.*] Do you want to know what I was really thinking?

JHILA: Yes.

MASUD: I was thinking of us, a long time ago. At the cinema.

JHILA: Masud.

MASUD: It felt the same.

JHILA: Yes. Because we have to say goodbye.

MASUD: Driving off into the sunset in Hamid's flash car…

JHILA: Don't.

MASUD: I'm teasing.

JHILA: Please wait until it's safe.

MASUD: There is no safe time. Just think—you'll have the whole room to yourselves again!

JHILA: I'd have stayed at my mother's whether you were here or not.

MASUD: [*nodding*] Hamid loves you.

JHILA: [*checking* AMIR] He doesn't listen to what I want.

MASUD: So you're going to give up on him?

JHILA: I don't know.

MASUD: If you run away what will you achieve? You'll still be in a mess and you'll have left behind your love.

JHILA: If I stay and fight for it I risk killing it.

MASUD: It's worth the risk.

JHILA: I don't know what to do.

MASUD: When you're sure about what you want you'll just do it.

    HAMID *enters.*

HAMID: If we're going, we've got to go now.

MASUD: Did you call Mr Darabi?

HAMID: Yeah.

MASUD: What did he say?

HAMID: It's not what he said. I don't trust him.

MASUD: You're as bad as Jhila. I met him once—he's all right.

HAMID: Stay here. At the weekend I can drive you to the border.

MASUD: No. It's time for me to go.

    He takes a gun from the bag and gives the remainder to HAMID.

You sure about this?

    He puts on his shoes.

HAMID: Reza said he can dispose of some. I'll hide the rest.

JHILA: Look, what harm can it do to stay a few more days?

MASUD: It's time for me to go. You've both been very kind to me.

    He strokes AMIR's *head and hugs* JHILA.

Cheer up—this is the way we always do things. Have faith.

JHILA: Goodbye.

MASUD: Come on, Hamid.

JHILA: [*to* HAMID] Be careful.

    They leave. She watches from a window.

AMIR: Mum!

JHILA: Shh, don't cry, don't cry.

◆ ◆ ◆ ◆ ◆

SCENE TWELVE

A street in a nearby town.

HAMID: This is the corner where you must wait. Mr Darabi said to hold
    the rose in your right hand like a gift. Where is it?

MASUD: I've left it in the car. Quick, go and get it.

HAMID: Are you okay?

MASUD: Yes.

HAMID: Look natural.

MASUD: Just get the rose, Hamid.

HAMID: Yes, right.

> *He goes.* MASUD *takes two glass capsules from a handkerchief and puts them under his tongue.*

[*Returning with a rose*] Here. Shit—I don't like all these people hanging around.

MASUD: It's the middle of Tehran.

HAMID: This rose is like a bloody signpost. Let's just go, wait an hour, then phone Darabi to check him out. If we're happy we can arrange another time.

MASUD: I'm going, Hamid. Now get back to the car. Quickly.

HAMID: Ring us from France.

> *He leaves.* MASUD *walks to the corner and waits.* MR DARABI *approaches.*

MR DARABI: Masud Amini?

MASUD: Yes. Mr Darabi?

> *They shake hands.*

MR DARABI: I'm sorry.

> MASUD *is grabbed by a* GUARD.

GUARD ONE: Spit it out! Spit it out!

> MASUD *swallows one capsule and bites on the other.*

Syringe! He's bitten it.

> *Another* GUARD *enters and before* MASUD *hits the ground he plunges a syringe into his arm.* MASUD *drops the rose.*

You've got to be quicker than that.

> *They drag him off. The rose is left behind.* AMIR *picks it up and stares at it.*

◆ ◆ ◆ ◆ ◆

SCENE THIRTEEN

The streets.

HAMID *is running. Loud banging. The women are not seen. Their voices come from the darkness, out of* HAMID*'s memory.*

NEDA: Hamid! It's Neda! Wake up. Let me in.

HAMID: What's wrong?

NEDA: They've arrested Reza.

JHILA: Why?

NEDA: He said you must get away quickly. They know about the guns. She weeps.

HAMID: Who told them?

NEDA: Some man. The man Reza sold the guns to.

HAMID: He sold them?

NEDA: I'm sorry! What will they do to him?

JHILA: Hamid, get out of here. Run!

HAMID: Hide the guns! Do it now, understand?

NEDA: Run, run! Find a safe place, Hamid!

JHILA: Run!

HAMID *stops running and presses a door intercom.*

VOICE: Hello?

HAMID: Ali! It's Hamid. I'm in trouble. Can I stay for a couple of nights?

The door opens. GUARD ONE *presses a gun against his chest,* GUARD TWO *against the back of his neck.*

GUARD ONE: Don't move.

He forces his hand into HAMID*'s mouth.*

Spit it out!

HAMID: Spit what out?

GUARD TWO: Where's the cyanide?

HAMID: I don't have cyanide—

GUARD ONE: You all have it.

HAMID: You've made a mistake.

GUARD ONE: Take him in.

HAMID: You've made a mistake!

They throw him down.

◆ ◆ ◆ ◆ ◆

SCENE FOURTEEN

Hamid and Jhila's room.

JHILA *lays out* HAMID*'s clothes.*

JHILA: Don't touch, Amir. Daddy might need these in the morning.

> *She refolds the trousers that* AMIR *has touched.* AMIR *touches her arm.*

◆ ◆ ◆ ◆ ◆

SCENE FIFTEEN

> *An interrogation room in prison, Tehran.*

HAMID: I need water.

AHMAD: Don't worry, everything's all right.

HAMID: Please, I really need to drink, and wash my face.

AHMAD: Soon, soon.

HAMID: How long am I going to be kept here?

AHMAD: Just a few questions, then you can go.

> AHMAD *sits, lights a cigarette and offers one to* HAMID, *who accepts, although* AHMAD *never lights it.* AHMAD *leafs through a file.*

Why are you in trouble?

HAMID: I don't know—I'm not in trouble.

AHMAD: [*reading*] 'Hello, it's Hamid. I'm in trouble, can I stay for a couple of nights?'

HAMID: Ah yes—I did say that, at my friend's house. It's personal—my wife and I—things aren't so good.

AHMAD: That's a pity. She beautiful?

HAMID: I think so.

AHMAD: Have you and your wife had a guest staying at your house?

HAMID: You mean recently?

> AHMAD *nods.*

Yeah—we had a friend with us for a while.

AHMAD: And what was his name?

HAMID *hesitates.*

What was his name?

HAMID: Masud Amini.

AHMAD: Why did he have a gun?

HAMID: I never saw a gun.

AHMAD: He gave a gun to your brother-in-law, Reza Afshar.

HAMID: I don't know anything about that.

AHMAD: Why was he staying at your house?

HAMID: He's an old university friend. He came to see us.

> AHMAD *takes* HAMID*'s cigarette and puts out his own as the* INTERROGATOR *enters.*

INTERROGATOR: Sit down. Why was Masud Amini staying at your house?

HAMID: I told this man—he's an old friend. He just came to visit. He had no other friends in Tehran.

INTERROGATOR: Why did he have guns?

HAMID: I never knew about any guns.

INTERROGATOR: Liar! Who are you connected to in the Mojahedin?

HAMID: Nobody—I'm not connected to anybody.

AHMAD: [*quietly*] Mr Parsi, we're not stupid. Reza has told us all about you and Masud.

INTERROGATOR: You were hiding him in your house. You emptied his shit in a bucket, Mojahedin scum!

HAMID: I'm not Mojahedin—I was just helping a friend.

AHMAD: [*quietly*] There's no point protecting him, Hamid. He's dead.

INTERROGATOR: He ate his own shit, your friend Masud.

AHMAD: [*close to* HAMID] He didn't bite his second cyanide capsule when he was arrested, he swallowed it, so he could retrieve it later. In the toilet.

INTERROGATOR: You are what you eat.

> *He chuckles.*

AHMAD: If you've swallowed a capsule, Hamid, please don't get any ideas. I'll be in the toilet with you.

INTERROGATOR: Who are your contacts?

HAMID: I don't have any.

INTERROGATOR: Take your shoes off.
HAMID: What?
INTERROGATOR: Now!

> HAMID *obeys*. AHMAD *takes off* HAMID*'s jacket.*

HAMID: What are you doing?
AHMAD: [*privately to* HAMID] I'm sorry.

> HAMID *struggles as* AHMAD *places him face down.* AHMAD *sits astride him and draws his chin up high.*

INTERROGATOR: What size shoe do you take?
HAMID: What—I don't…
INTERROGATOR: What size shoe?!
HAMID: Forty-three.
INTERROGATOR: Again!
HAMID: Forty-three!
INTERROGATOR: Louder!
HAMID: Forty-three, forty-three!
INTERROGATOR: Right.

> AHMAD *stuffs the jacket into* HAMID*'s mouth, ties it behind his head, and pulls at the jacket to lift up his head further, while the* INTERROGATOR *produces a baton.*

We'll make it ninety-three.

◆ ◆ ◆ ◆ ◆

SCENE SIXTEEN

Jhila and Hamid's room.

NEDA *is sitting in her chador.* JHILA *enters, also in a chador.*

JHILA: Neda?
NEDA: Is Hamid all right?
JHILA: They say he's definitely in there. What about Reza?
NEDA: They say he's okay.

> *They tear off the chadors.*

I lost you—when they sent me to that other room.

JHILA: Why did the guards move you out of my queue?

NEDA: Because I sat on a chair. A man was called in so I took his seat. They pointed a gun at me and said I was turned on by the heat of his arse! He was at least ninety! [*She laughs. Pause.*] I'm sorry, Jhila—I don't know why Reza sold the guns.

JHILA: He should have hidden them, like us.

NEDA: I told him to throw them away.

JHILA: He never lets a deal go by.

NEDA: I've said I'm sorry.

JHILA: Look what he's done to us all.

NEDA: Hamid started this!

JHILA: Reza couldn't wait to show off and make some money!

NEDA: You let Masud in—you were risking all our lives—

JHILA: We're still here, aren't we?

> *Pause.*

NEDA: A woman in the jail told me it could be years. My aunt said I should look for a new husband.

JHILA: For God's sake, don't start crying! Neda—we knew what we were doing. All of us.

NEDA: I didn't. Nobody asked me what I thought.

GUARD ONE: [*offstage*] Hurry up!

JHILA: Hello? Who's there?

> HAMID *enters, shuffling.*

Hamid.

HAMID: Hi, Jhila.

> JHILA *goes to him as* AHMAD *and* GUARDS *follow* HAMID *into the room.*

JHILA: Are they going to release you?

> HAMID *shakes his head.*

HAMID: They want the guns. Where did you hide them? It's all right. They know everything. You can say.

JHILA: What's happened to your feet?

GUARD ONE: He fell down the stairs.

AHMAD: Please, answer the question.

JHILA: I hid them in the sewer. Under the footbridge across the road.

What have they done to you?

HAMID: It's all right, Jhila.

> AHMAD *leaves.*

[*To* GUARD ONE] You said I could change my shirt?

GUARD ONE: Hurry up.

> *The* GUARD *looks out the window.* HAMID *struggles with the buttons on his shirt.*

JHILA: I've kept one ready.

HAMID: Where's Amir?

JHILA: With my mother. I had my final exam.

> *She helps him.*

HAMID: I'll do it.

> JHILA *fetches the clean shirt.* HAMID *takes off his shirt.* NEDA *gasps to see his lacerated back.* HAMID *edges away to shield his back from* JHILA, *but she sees it in the mirror. She moves closer, in shock, then turns to look at the cuts and weals on* HAMID's *skin.*

JHILA: [*to* GUARD ONE, *distraught*] Did you do this?

GUARD ONE: There's ice—he slipped. Cut his back.

NEDA: Do you think she's as stupid as you are?

HAMID: Neda, please!

> JHILA *silently and carefully puts the shirt on* HAMID.

AHMAD: [*returning*] The guns weren't there, but it's all right—your neighbour says she saw the guards take them off some kids.

GUARD ONE: We'll check that out. Come on.

> JHILA *momentarily rests her head against* HAMID. *He breaks away.*

HAMID: Don't cry.

JHILA: [*dry-eyed*] I'm not.

HAMID: I'll see you.

AHMAD: Don't worry, he'll be back in three days, you'll see.

AMIR: Mum and I went back to Grandma's. She woke us all up in the night. I heard her telling Grandma that she'd had a bad dream. She didn't believe what the guards said. We must wait, said Grandma.

Mum said yes, we must wait. And so we did, while those three days turned into three years.

♦ ♦ ♦ ♦ ♦

SCENE SEVENTEEN

Brendan's office. May, 1992.

STEPHANIE: Sit down, everyone.

JHILA: We thank you for get us out of prison.

STEPHANIE: Sorry, it took three weeks to get a different Magistrate. Now listen, we've had some good news this morning—the diplomats have dropped the money and passport allegations. The police couldn't find any evidence.

HAMID: Of course—we never went near that safe.

STEPHANIE: So things are looking up.

HAMID: Is good.

STEPHANIE: And we've booked you onto the twelve-fifteen flight back to Brisbane. You can get straight back to work.

HAMID: But where is Kamran?

STEPHANIE: There's a taxi booked to pick him up at the hospital. You know, you don't have to take him in. There are services available—

HAMID: Now he is so sick, we have to help him.

BRENDAN *enters.*

Brendan, how are you?

They shake hands.

BRENDAN: Hamid. Jhila. [*To* AMIR] G'day mate. [*To* STEPHANIE] Can I have a word?

STEPHANIE: What's the matter?

BRENDAN: We're back to square one. The charge is going to be conspiracy.

STEPHANIE: What?

BRENDAN: They're going for maximum damage.

STEPHANIE: That's ridiculous.

BRENDAN: The book's being thrown at them… from a great height.

AMIR: What's up?

Eugene Gilfedder as Hamid (background) and Yalin Ozucelik as Amir in the 1998 Matrix Theatre Company production at the La Boite Theatre, Brisbane. (Photo: Rob Maccoll)

STEPHANIE: I'll tell them.

BRENDAN: No, I'll do it. I've been to see the Magistrate. As you know, we were facing up to the simple charges of damage to diplomatic property and injury to personnel. But now the Prosecution has altered the charge. They're going to try to prove that you conspired to plan the attack.

HAMID: No way, no way.

JHILA: [*overlapping*] What?

BRENDAN: Well, that's the charge we'll have to answer—that you had a common purpose. Whether we like it or not.

HAMID: Why are they changing minds?

BRENDAN: The Government's trying to make an example of you. To show the voters, and the Iranians, how tough they are on terrorism. Your plea will now have to change to 'not guilty'.

HAMID: What? So I cannot say to Judge—I am guilty of spraying paint, I am guilty of breaking office—I am sorry, please punish me, and I am absolved. I cannot say that?

BRENDAN: No, you can't. And I warn you, the new charge carries a much harsher sentence.

HAMID: How long?

BRENDAN: Jhila should be okay, but for you, maximum ten years.

AMIR: It's all right, Mum, Brendan will get us off, won't you?

BRENDAN: I can't promise anything, Amir.

AMIR: You've got to now!

BRENDAN: Hamid, I have to say that if you're found guilty, the Judge will also be within his rights to order that you be deported.

HAMID: He can do that?

BRENDAN: Yep.

AMIR: No!

STEPHANIE: It's unlikely to come to that.

HAMID: I thought, here in Australia, you have no death sentence.

AMIR: How can they be sent back for smashing a bottle or spraying paint? You call that justice?

BRENDAN: It's the law.

AMIR: Then you've got to do something about it! If he goes back he's dead!

BRENDAN: Oh, come on—

AMIR: You're supposed to be the best! You don't look like it!

HAMID: Amir!

AMIR: Someone's got to stand up to these bastards. Dad, you're an Australian citizen, they can't do this to you.

BRENDAN: Amir, we haven't lost yet. Calm down.

AMIR: Shit.

> *He goes to the window.*

STEPHANIE: Listen. There's plenty of evidence to prove that you didn't conspire to attack the Embassy. There's a good case to be made. You'll just have to be patient.

AMIR: How long for? Days or years?

STEPHANIE: Amir, you're not helping your parents, just calm down.

JHILA: You have no idea.

STEPHANIE: Jhila, you must go home, get back to work.

> AHMAD *appears.* HAMID *looks at him.*

Okay? Hamid?

> HAMID *doesn't respond.*

HAMID: I need water.

STEPHANIE: Hamid?

AHMAD: Everything will be all right.

BRENDAN: Leave everything to us.

HAMID: Please, I really need to drink and wash my face.

AHMAD: Soon, soon…

> AHMAD *and another* GUARD *place* HAMID *in the coffin-like cage.*

JHILA: They have seventy-four tortures in Iran. More. All different. Same as Nazis did. That is where they got them from. They put him in coffin—they call it 'coffin and cage'—a tiny cage all day, coffin all night. He has ten minutes for toilet, washing, food—all that. The beatings never stop. No trial. He is there, four hundred twenty-five days. If we must go back, they will kill him.

> *She goes.*

STEPHANIE: [*to* AMIR] Look after her.

AMIR: Sorry about losing it before.

BRENDAN: Don't worry about it.

STEPHANIE: We'll sort things out.

> AMIR *joins* JHILA.

Every way I look at it… we're fucked.

BRENDAN: [*overlapping*] … we're fucked.

STEPHANIE: 'Common purpose'. How did they get it past the Magistrate?

BRENDAN: It's not his call. Foreign Affairs refused the diplomats' request for police protection. They said: (a) the raid wouldn't happen, and (b) it would cost too much. So when it happens—

STEPHANIE: —they look like dickheads.

BRENDAN: Iran is our biggest export market in the Middle East. We've got to keep them happy.

STEPHANIE: They've got us over a barrel.

BRENDAN: So both governments are going to protect the diplomats at all costs.

> *Pause.*

STEPHANIE: They wouldn't deport them, would they? [*Pause.*] Are you staying on this?

BRENDAN: It's got a whole lot more interesting, hasn't it?

STEPHANIE: Is that a yes?

BRENDAN: Let's talk about it over dinner.

> *The* GUARDS *take away the 'coffin', leaving* HAMID *on the floor.* KAMRAN *kneels beside him and rubs his feet.* STEPHANIE *nods gently at* BRENDAN *and they move away together.*

AMIR: The other prisoners have ointment for his feet. It's a beautiful moment for him. To be with people. Like he's been given the world again.

◆ ◆ ◆ ◆ ◆

SCENE EIGHTEEN

The take-away shop, Brisbane. May, 1992.

In the garden HAMID *tears at some rose bushes.* KAMRAN *watches.* JHILA *watches* HAMID *from a window.*

AMIR: I'm taking Dad a beer—do you want one?

JHILA: No.

AMIR: What's he doing?

JHILA: Trying to pull up the roses.

AMIR: Why?

JHILA: They died while we were away.

AMIR: They're not dead, Mum—they just need water.

> *He runs to* HAMID *in the garden.*

Dad—Dad, don't do that—they're not dead. The roots are fine.

HAMID: All the flowers and leaves have gone.

AMIR: But the roots are okay. You paid a lot for them, Dad. Please leave them. We'll just trim off the dead stuff and water them. Yeah?

> HAMID *sits.* AMIR *hands him the beer.*

HAMID: [*looking at the can*] Didn't they have any heavies?

AMIR: Mum bought it.

> HAMID *gives it to* AMIR *who drinks with enjoyment.*

Cat's piss.

> *He sees* JHILA *with a watering can nearby and quickly hides the beer.*

HAMID: Look at the sky—beautiful.

JHILA: [*watering the roses*] They didn't want to come up, did they?

HAMID: He thinks they're still alive.

JHILA: I think so too. Don't you, Kamran? They just need a bit of help.

HAMID: I don't think we'll see them bloom again.

> *He looks at his hands.*

AMIR: What have you done? Mum—look at his hands!

JHILA: It doesn't matter. It's blood in the soil that makes roses red. You'll see.

> *They drink and look at the sky.* KAMRAN *watches.* HAMID *snaps his fingers near* KAMRAN*'s face and lies down, arms outstretched.*

> *Blackout.*

END OF ACT ONE

ACT TWO

SCENE ONE

The take-away shop, Brisbane. September, 1993.

HAMID *plays his flute, plaintively.* KAMRAN *stares at him.*

AMIR: It's over a year since the raid. We're still waiting for the case to get to court. Hardly anyone comes into the shop now. We've lost them. It was closed for too long. It feels like a kind of nightmare, this waiting, but we never wake up and it goes on and on with us still in the papers and everyone 'round here thinking we're terrorists. They call me Saddam Hussein on the school bus.

JHILA: [*offstage*] Hamid! Where's the bread? And you've forgotten the bins again!

HAMID: Shit.

JHILA: [*entering*] If the health inspector comes, that's it—we're closed. You've got to wake up.

HAMID: All right.

JHILA: What's the matter with you?

> HAMID *glances at* KAMRAN.

Never mind Kamran—answer me!

HAMID: He's not deaf.

JHILA: He's in his own world, he doesn't care what we say.

HAMID: He listens.

JHILA: I can't speak to my own husband in my own house.

> KAMRAN *wanders off.* HAMID *follows him.*

Hamid!

HAMID: I can't leave him on his own.

JHILA: You'd think he was a baby.

HAMID: He was down here in the night, with a knife. You want me to let him get on with it?

JHILA: Oh God.

She turns and bumps into KAMRAN *on her way out.*

HAMID: [*lifting the flute, but pausing*] Shall I open up?

JHILA: There's not much point if there's no food to sell. Another day we'll be late opening.

She exits.

KAMRAN: You're a mess. You're a loser.

HAMID: But I'm still one step ahead of you.

HAMID *starts playing again, tentatively.* AMIR *sits beside him.*

AMIR: [*of* KAMRAN] I wish he wasn't here. He's weird. He follows Dad around like a dog that's always fixing you with its eyes. You don't know if it's asking you for something, or blaming you for something, or if it just wants to tear your throat out.

KAMRAN: You're in trouble.

JHILA: [*offstage*] Hamid. We've got to be ready earlier.

AMIR: I sit like this a lot.

JHILA: [*offstage*] I'll get the bread from now on.

AMIR: To remind Dad that I exist.

JHILA: [*offstage*] But you must be up by five.

AMIR: He's always somewhere else.

JHILA: [*offstage*] You just have to wake yourself up, Hamid!

◆ ◆ ◆ ◆ ◆

SCENE TWO

The prison, Tehran. 1983.

An insistent loud banging. PRISONERS *lie asleep on the floor.*

GUARD: Wake up you fucking bastards! Up!

The PRISONERS *jump to their feet, suddenly alert.*

PRISONER ONE: It's 5 a.m. Go, go, go!

The PRISONERS *hurriedly stow their blankets, then rush to their first tasks of the morning routine.*

AMIR: The cell is six metres by six metres, and Dad's one of ninety men living in it.

The stage is alive with PRISONERS *purposefully crossing, circling and crossing—time and time again.* HAMID *stands amongst them, unsure. A* PRISONER *pulls imaginary toothpaste from his pocket and one by one the others scrub at their teeth as they move to the showers. They shunt regimentally along the line of showers, fully-dressed, arms raised, before heading to the toilet cubicle where they squat or stand for a second before continuing the routine. Once the routine has fully established,* PRISONER ONE *produces a watch.* HAMID *is confused.*

PRISONER ONE: Go, go, go!

He opens a cubicle door open for a PRISONER *who runs in.* PRISONERS *continue to run through the showers, fully-clothed, and to brush their teeth.*

Come on, come on!

The occupant emerges and races to the toothpaste dispenser, who hands it over and races to the shower. Another runs from the shower to brush his teeth, another to the cubicle. HAMID *collides with* PRISONER TWO *entering the cubicle.*

PRISONER TWO: Shower! Shower!

He shoves HAMID *towards the shower.* HAMID *starts to strip off but is shunted under the water by the others.*

PRISONER THREE: Get in!
PRISONER FOUR: Why are you undressed?
HAMID: We're in the shower! Why are you dressed?
PRISONER FOUR: Wash your clothes.
HAMID: Oh!

HAMID *turns to fetch his shirt, bumping into others.*

PRISONER THREE: Get out of the way!
HAMID: Okay, okay, I'm new, all right?

The routine continues.

PRISONER FIVE: [*emerging from the cubicle*] I've broken the record!

The PRISONERS *clap.* HAMID *brushes his teeth with a finger.*

KAMRAN: [*smiling*] You'll get used to it. Toilet next. Fast! Or you won't make it.

HAMID *races to the cubicle.*

Hey—tell your wife to bring you a toothbrush!

HAMID: Thank you!

> HAMID's *turn comes and the door slams behind him. A queue forms outside the cubicle.*

PRISONER SIX: Come on!

PRISONER TWO: We're going to miss our food.

PRISONER ONE: Time's nearly up!

HAMID: I've only just got in!

PRISONER FIVE: Tell that to the guards.

PRISONER TWO: [*to* HAMID] Come on.

PRISONER ONE: You've got ten seconds left.

> *The cubicle door opens.*

HAMID: I can't go.

> *The queue groans.*

What do I do now?

PRISONER FIVE: There's food in the cell. Get a partner. Look, sorry— you'll learn to shit fast.

> *The* PRISONERS *sit in pairs, as if to share a bowl of food, but remain motionless until it's their turn to exercise.*

KAMRAN: Over here! You can share my bowl.

HAMID: Thanks.

KAMRAN: Five hundred prisoners, six toilets, ten minutes.

HAMID: It's absurd.

KAMRAN: We don't mean to be rude to you. If we run over time, the guards give us hell all day. There's a bucket over there. Distasteful, I know—but it's a last resort.

> *The* PRISONERS *walk around the room in pairs, turn by turn.*

I'm Kamran.

HAMID: Hamid. How long have you been in here?

KAMRAN: Two years. They pulled me out of a lecture I was giving at university one day. No explanation, no trial—

HAMID: After two years?

KAMRAN: I'm lucky. That man's been waiting for three.

REZA *taps* HAMID *on the shoulder.*

REZA: Welcome to the Tehran Hilton.

HAMID: Reza! Are you okay?

REZA: Never better. You wouldn't believe the contacts I've made in here!

HAMID: You know Kamran?

REZA: We all know Kamran.

HAMID: Reza's my brother-in-law.

KAMRAN: It's our turn to walk.

REZA: Go, go!

    KAMRAN *and* HAMID *walk around the room.*

KAMRAN: You'll eat with me from now on. If the guards are around don't talk. Or laugh. Your beatings will get worse.

HAMID: I can take the beatings—it's their insults I can't stand.

KAMRAN: You've got to make your mind as tough as your body. And never change your story. Not by a word. It could mean five years on your sentence. And practise what you've said every day.

GUARD: Get off your arses, you lazy bastards, prayers.

    HAMID *and* KAMRAN *continue to walk to the prayer hall, while the other* PRISONERS *take off their shoes and assemble.*

REZA: Come on. It's special prayer day.

HAMID: I don't know how to pray. What do I do?

REZA: Don't ask me, I'm a Communist.

HAMID: Then what do you actually do?

REZA: Just follow Kamran. He's a good Muslim.

    They take off their shoes.

KAMRAN: Better to follow me than him, Hamid—whatever you believe.

HAMID: Thanks.

    They join the mass of people.

God, there must be a thousand people in here.

KAMRAN: Shshshsh— [*Whispering*] You're not allowed to talk.

    All kneel. Devotions begin. HAMID *loses his balance, his head heavily butting the bottom of the man in front of him.*

HAMID: Shit! Sorry.

Eugene Gilfedder as Hamid in the 1998 Matrix Theatre Company production at the La Boite Theatre, Brisbane. (Photo: Rob Maccoll)

KAMRAN: Sshh!

> REZA *and* HAMID *stifle laughter. The devotions continue. All kneel.*

HAMID: [*poking his head up, whispering*] How long have we been here?

REZA: [*poking his head up, whispering*] An hour.

HAMID: How much longer to go?

REZA: Another hour.

HAMID: I'm in trouble.

> *All kneel up, all kneel down.*

I need to use the bucket.

REZA: Well, you're fucked.

> *An unseen* GUARD *gently weeps and wails, some* PRISONERS *join in.*

HAMID: What's happening now?

REZA: The guards like it if you cry!

> *The* PRISONERS *rise, forming a circle around* REZA *and* HAMID. *The wailing builds to passionate levels.* HAMID *is astounded, finding the scene unnerving.* REZA *laughs.* HAMID *laughs with him. The wailing quietens. The laughter subsides.* KAMRAN *frowns. They all kneel. Silence. The backs of* REZA *and* HAMID *shake.*

Not long to go now.

HAMID: Don't talk about it.

> *They race to the shoes as everyone prepares to leave.*

KAMRAN: [*catching up*] Do you think no one noticed you laughing?

REZA: I've told you before, Kamran—it's nothing against you.

KAMRAN: No, it's against Allah.

REZA: The guards need the piss taken out of them.

KAMRAN: You must remember that we pray from our hearts.

HAMID: Kamran, I apologise. I'm sorry if we offended you.

KAMRAN: Please don't do it again.

> REZA *scoffs.* KAMRAN *moves off. A* PRISONER *knocks* HAMID *to the ground.*

PRISONER ONE: Next time you laugh in prayers, I'll beat the shit out of you.

He exits. AHMAD *hoists* HAMID *to his feet.*

AHMAD: You okay?

HAMID: Yeah.

AHMAD: Be careful when you have fun in here.

HAMID: Fun?

AHMAD: [*smiling*] What's your name?

HAMID: Hamid Parsi.

AHMAD: Call me Hassan. You married?

HAMID: Yeah.

AHMAD: It's bad for a man to be apart from his wife.

HAMID *nods.*

She beautiful?

HAMID: You saw her.

AHMAD *frowns.*

You came to my house.

AHMAD: Ah, yes. She hid some guns. Yes, beautiful. Aren't you worried about her being out there on her own?

HAMID: She's with my family.

AHMAD *nods, then smiles.*

AHMAD: If there's anything you want, I might be able to get it for you.

HAMID: Right… thank you.

AHMAD *wanders off smiling.*

REZA: I get cigarettes off him. If you stay on the right side of him he's fine. Watch this.

AHMAD: [*to* KAMRAN] You going to give me your shoes?

REZA: He does it all the time.

AHMAD: Come on. Give me your shoes.

KAMRAN *shakes his head.*

You don't need them in here… I'll give you four cigarettes for them.

KAMRAN: No thank you.

AHMAD: [*kicking at* KAMRAN's *feet*] Come on… [*Smiling at* REZA *and* HAMID] He's holding out for a packet of twenty!

REZA *laughs.*

[*To* KAMRAN] Maybe tomorrow I'll take them.

He viciously kicks KAMRAN*'s feet.*

HAMID: Why's he doing this?
REZA: They're good shoes!

AHMAD *leaves.*

HAMID: [*to* KAMRAN] Shouldn't you just give them to him?
KAMRAN: I've given him a ring and my watch. He's not getting these.
HAMID: Just to get him off your back?
KAMRAN: He likes to play games.
HAMID: What do you mean?

KAMRAN *shrugs.* HAMID *looks at* REZA.

They are good shoes!

♦ ♦ ♦ ♦ ♦

SCENE THREE

The take-away shop.

HAMID *sits on the floor.* KAMRAN *watches.*

AMIR: [*entering*] Dad? Dad, they're here.
HAMID: What?
AMIR: The trial date's set.
HAMID: Thank God.
AMIR: Mum says quick!
HAMID: Kamran, our lawyers are here. Come on.
KAMRAN: You don't need a lawyer for what you did.
HAMID: [*to* AMIR] Stay with him.
AMIR: Dad!
HAMID: He's bad today. He can't be left on his own.
AMIR: All right.

HAMID *leaves. Pause.*

Do you want to play cricket?

Pause.

JHILA: [*entering with* BRENDAN *and* STEPHANIE] You are early.

> *She takes off her shoes.*

STEPHANIE: Yes—sorry.

JHILA: But we happy to see you—is not easy, this long time.

STEPHANIE: No.

JHILA: Hamid is coming. Could I ask, could you take off shoes please?

STEPHANIE: Oh, yes, sorry—

BRENDAN: I thought only the Japanese took their shoes off.

STEPHANIE: Don't be stupid, lots of cultures do, don't they, Jhila?

JHILA: No—is best carpet, from Iran.

STEPHANIE: Oh.

> JHILA *puts their shoes away.*

AMIR: Brendan's only on the case to keep Stephanie around. I sussed that out months ago. Mum and Dad think he's doing his best for them. But I'm not sure anymore.

HAMID: Brendan! Stephanie! It's beautiful you here. Let's have a drink.

STEPHANIE: No, thank you, Hamid.

JHILA: [*to* HAMID, *in Farsi, resentfully*] You've cheered up.

HAMID: Oh, come on… this is time for celebrate.

STEPHANIE: Really, no.

JHILA: [*in Farsi*] They don't want a drink.

HAMID: Okay, okay, work first, yes?

STEPHANIE: Shouldn't we get Kamran?

HAMID: No—he's not, you know…

> STEPHANIE *nods.*

BRENDAN: Kamran's home and dry. Right. The trial starts in four weeks. I just want to run through this from the beginning.

HAMID: Sure, sure—this is great—you sure you don't want a drink?

BRENDAN: Not just now. Right. You're being charged with conspiring to cause damage to diplomatic property and personnel—or acting with a common purpose. You remember?

HAMID: Yes, yes…

BRENDAN: [*rapidly*] Now, the Prosecution's definition of 'common purpose' is pretty complicated. They're going to try and prove, on both counts, that you acted jointly with at least one other accused who also, on the evidence available, is proved to have acted jointly either with you or at least one of the other people in the raid. Are you with me?

HAMID: Hang on, hang on… no, not really.

BRENDAN: You and Jhila, and at least one other person, must be proved to be jointly guilty, by way of acting with a common purpose, or by way of aiding and abetting—

STEPHANIE: That means helping the others to do criminal things, or them helping you to do them.

HAMID: [*not understanding*] Okay…

BRENDAN: So we only have to prove that you acted individually and spontaneously to make the attack. And in this case 'attack' means 'any kind of hostile aggression including, but not limited to, physical or verbal intimidation, aggression or assault'.

STEPHANIE: Brendan.

BRENDAN: But you don't have to worry about that.

JHILA: I not understand.

BRENDAN: [*to* JHILA] When you threw the bottle, whatever they ask you, you say—I did it alone, no one was watching, no one told me to do it. And that is all you say. So don't start telling them you did it because you hate the Ayatollah, okay?

JHILA: But that is true why I throw bottle.

KAMRAN *enters with* AMIR.

BRENDAN: The jury doesn't need to know that.

Pause.

HAMID: Please, Brendan, I'm not quite understanding this. So what you mean, when I tell my story—

BRENDAN: Your story's not important.

HAMID: What are you saying? I cannot speak?

BRENDAN: Look, we've heard what happened to you. It's terrible, but—

HAMID: Court is not interested in truth?

BRENDAN: Only in answer to these very particular charges.

HAMID: [*to* JHILA, *in Farsi*] This is crazy.

AMIR: Kamran wanted to come in.

HAMID: [*to* STEPHANIE] You think this?

She looks down.

We want jury to believe raid was spontaneous, yes? Then we must tell story for them to know how it happen.

STEPHANIE *looks at* BRENDAN *archly.*

Simple!

BRENDAN: Hamid, you'll get emotional and you'll make mistakes.

HAMID: Do you think we can't do talking ourself?

BRENDAN: I'm not saying that—

HAMID: Do you think we are children to shut up?

AMIR: [*to* BRENDAN] You can't do this!

KAMRAN: [*in Farsi*] Tell them the truth, Hamid.

He chuckles.

HAMID: [*to* KAMRAN, *in Farsi*] Not now, please.

AMIR: [*to* BRENDAN] You never want to listen to him, Brendan.

BRENDAN: All right. What do you want to say?

HAMID: [*distracted*] Pardon?

BRENDAN: What do you want to say?

KAMRAN: [*in Farsi*] Tell them the truth.

HAMID: [*in Farsi*] Be quiet! [*To* BRENDAN] Sorry, you mean now?

BRENDAN: Yeah, just like you're in the dock. In trial. I'm listening.

HAMID: Well. I say, ladies and gentlemen in jury, we have, as I am telling you, many bad experience in Iran from the regime there. Then we hear of terrible bombing of Mojahedin—

BRENDAN: You can't say—

HAMID: Yes, yes I know—I must not say Mojahedin—

BRENDAN: You start talking like that, they say 'He's a terrorist'!

STEPHANIE: Oh, God.

BRENDAN: We've been down this road before—

HAMID: Okay, so I say we come to Embassy to protest with family, no weapons, nothing. Then, jury, we see gate open for car, and one after one—

BRENDAN: And they've got you!

KAMRAN *laughs.*

HAMID: What?

BRENDAN: As soon as you say one person went in and you saw and followed, you are guilty of acting with a 'common purpose'.

STEPHANIE *grunts*.

Something wrong, Stephanie?

HAMID: Okay, okay… and then we get to building, guy is there spraying fire thing at us—

KAMRAN: [*in Farsi*] What happened then, tell them that.

HAMID: —so we get mad and we run in—

BRENDAN: Got you again. You're saying 'we', 'us'—

STEPHANIE: He could practise.

AMIR: Yeah. You're making it hard for him. He can't think.

KAMRAN: [*in Farsi*] You tell the rest of it, Hamid.

HAMID: [*in Farsi*] Shut up! [*To* BRENDAN] You want to put handcuffs on my mouth!

JHILA: Hamid—

STEPHANIE: No decisions have to be made about anything yet, Hamid. Let's talk about the moment when you raised your spanner, remember?

KAMRAN: [*in English*] I remember.

STEPHANIE: Thank you, Kamran, but you weren't on the video at that point.

KAMRAN: [*in Farsi*] Tell her you remember.

HAMID: [*in Farsi*] Keep quiet!

JHILA: [*in Farsi*] What does he mean?

BRENDAN: Speak English please.

STEPHANIE: Now the video shows you raising the spanner and lunging forward. The whole case could rest on this moment, Hamid. It's very important you tell us exactly what happened.

HAMID: [*in English*] Diplomat throw bin at me. I turn—

STEPHANIE: Just a minute. He threw the bin at you?

HAMID: It nearly hit me—

STEPHANIE: Why didn't you tell us before?

KAMRAN: [*in Farsi*] It must have slipped your mind.

STEPHANIE: [*to* BRENDAN] Self defence!

BRENDAN: But why were you lifting the spanner?

KAMRAN: [*in Farsi*] Good question.

BRENDAN: The Prosecution is going to say at that moment you were attacking the diplomat.

KAMRAN *laughs.*

HAMID: [*to* KAMRAN, *in Farsi*] Shut up!

BRENDAN: So what were you doing?

STEPHANIE: Go easy.

KAMRAN *continues to laugh.*

HAMID: [*to* KAMRAN] Shut up!

BRENDAN: What were you doing, Hamid? [*Pause.*] Do you understand me?

AMIR: Dad?

Pause.

STEPHANIE: Brilliant.

BRENDAN: Are you not talking to us now, Hamid?

Pause.

JHILA: He practises to keep mouth shut, for court.

BRENDAN: Okay. We'll come back in a couple of weeks.

AMIR: What's wrong, Dad? You've got to let him speak, Brendan!

BRENDAN: Sorry. If he wants to get off, this is the way it's got to be.

HAMID *storms out.*

STEPHANIE: Great. [*To* JHILA, *who is holding their shoes*] I'm sorry. If you need to talk…

BRENDAN: [*on the way out, to* JHILA] Your English is getting better.

JHILA: [*coldly*] Thank you.

BRENDAN: Think about what we've said. Talk to him.

JHILA: You give him hell.

She walks out.

STEPHANIE: [*outside*] Well done, Brendan, we now have a mute for a client.

BRENDAN: Fine by me.

STEPHANIE: So can we try my way now?

BRENDAN: We did that with the press conference. Where did that get us? Anyway, I didn't shut him up, Kamran did.

STEPHANIE: No he didn't. Did he?

AMIR: [*following them*] I told them you could fix things up. But you don't give a shit! Look what you've done to him!

STEPHANIE: Oh, come on, Amir.

AMIR: I know whose side you're on now. [*To* BRENDAN] We don't need a fucking trial, he's in prison already!

STEPHANIE: Amir, we're not trying—

AMIR: Why don't you just piss off? He'll be better off without you.

STEPHANIE: Please, let us explain.

AMIR: Just go!

BRENDAN: Come on, Stephanie.

> *They leave.*

AMIR: You're a prick, Brendan! [*To the audience*] I feel better after that. [*He goes to sit with* HAMID.] There's another prick on TV.

> HAMID *shines the hand-held light into* AHMAD'*s face.*

AHMAD: We are very pleased it comes to court at last. The Iranian Government is doing all it can to co-operate with the legal process to bring these terrorists to justice. We will see this through to the end to stop this kind of conspiracy—

> JHILA *turns off the television, by snatching away the light.*

HAMID: Hey, hey…

JHILA: [*in Farsi*] How many more times do you want to watch it? Amir, upstairs please. What's going on with Kamran?

> AMIR *reluctantly moves away.*

HAMID: Nothing.

JHILA: Why don't you talk to me? It's like there's a wall between us.

HAMID: Maybe we should give it up.

> *Pause.* JHILA *glances at* KAMRAN.

JHILA: [*whispering*] What? The shop? You mean the shop?

> HAMID *shrugs. He glances at* KAMRAN. *On another part of the stage* STEPHANIE *searches through documents.*

AMIR: I'm sitting in the dark on the stairs. Mum and Dad are sitting in the dark with the telly off. At last I'm like the other kids at school— I'm in a dysfunctional family!

JHILA: [*sitting next to* AMIR] When your father was in prison, in Iran, I went to the Shrine at Mashad. I fed the pigeons and said a prayer like you're supposed to. First, I prayed for the release of Uncle Reza—

AMIR: Why him?

JHILA: To show humility. You must leave the thing you really want until last, so as not to be selfish. Then I begged for your father to come to me. My tears fell down. The pigeons flew up.

AMIR: And the next day…

JHILA: [*nodding*] He was released.

AMIR: I don't believe in God.

JHILA: Just make a wish.

AMIR: Yeah, yeah.

◆ ◆ ◆ ◆ ◆

SCENE FOUR

The prison, Tehran.

AHMAD: I have a surprise for you. Over here.

HAMID: What's happening?

AHMAD: Your beautiful wife—she's coming to see you.

HAMID: What am I going to say to her?

AHMAD: I know what I'd say.

HAMID: I look like shit—I stink—

AHMAD: She won't smell you through the glass. Come on! Be happy. I went to a lot of trouble to arrange this.

HAMID: Oh, yeah…

AHMAD: Smile! If she loves you she won't care what you look like.

HAMID: Yeah.

AHMAD: You've got to show her you're still a man. So what are you going to say?

HAMID: I don't know.

AHMAD: Come on.

HAMID: I have to be—you know—with her—

AHMAD: [*offended*] Okay.

　　　He moves away. HAMID *waits.*

FATHER: Oh, God…

JHILA: Please, Father.

AMIR: We're on our first visit to the prison. Granddad insists on coming. At least he pays for the taxi. Where's Daddy?

JHILA: We'll see Daddy soon.

FATHER: This place. It's making me so depressed.

JHILA: You'll only have to be here for half an hour. [*To* AMIR] We can only see Daddy for a very little while, okay?

FATHER: That's a blessing, I say.

JHILA: He's your son!

FATHER: I should have stayed behind.

AMIR: Yes, Granddad, you should.

JHILA: Shh! [*To* FATHER] Try to cheer up before you see him.

FATHER: I'll try…

JHILA: We've waited so long.

AMIR: And we had to wait another four hours—with Granddad complaining.

JHILA: They're opening the door. Hamid! Hamid!

> HAMID *stands as* JHILA *makes her way to the visiting area.*

AHMAD: I forgot she was so skinny.

> *A* GUARD *hands* JHILA *a telephone.*

JHILA: Hamid!

AMIR: Daddy!

HAMID: Jhila! [*Pause.*] How are you doing?

JHILA: I can't hear you.

AHMAD: Pick up the phone!

> HAMID *is handed a telephone.*

HAMID: Hello. Can you hear me?

> *He waves at* AMIR *and smiles at his* FATHER.

JHILA: Hello.

HAMID: [*glancing at* AHMAD] How long have you been waiting?

FATHER: What did he say?

JHILA: Are you all right?

HAMID: Yeah.

JHILA: Hamid, you don't need to shout.

HAMID: Oh…

JHILA: Have they hurt you?

HAMID: No. No problems. Really. What's been happening at home?

JHILA: I passed my exam.

HAMID: Yes…? I was sending you good luck.

FATHER: I can't hear what he's saying!

JHILA: [*sighing*] Here.

> *She hands* FATHER *the phone.*

FATHER: [*shouting*] Hamid—hello! Hello!

HAMID: Dad, hello—

FATHER: Do you know how long we've been here? Four and a half hours! Can you believe that? This place—how can you stay here? Dirty. Disgusting place. Still, at least you're in Tehran. When are you coming home, son?

HAMID: They don't tell us—

FATHER: Getting enough to eat?

HAMID: Yeah—Dad, there's no need to shout—

FATHER: Good, good. Hey, listen, son. Don't worry about Jhila. I'm keeping an eye on her. I'm making sure no strange men come visiting—none of those university types. No funny business. Hurry home. Hurry home.

> *He passes the receiver to* JHILA.

JHILA: Hi.

HAMID: Is Dad all right?

JHILA: Yes.

HAMID: Jhila. This situation, it's no good.

JHILA: It doesn't matter.

HAMID: Some of these guys—they've been in here, maybe three or four years with no trial.

JHILA: It could be twenty, thirty years—I don't care.

HAMID: It's not fair on you.

JHILA: What do you think I am? [*Pause.*] Anyway, your father's looking after me.

GUARD: Children under five may visit their fathers for one minute.

JHILA: Amir—go see your Daddy. Go with the man.

> *She ushers the imaginary* AMIR *towards the* GUARD. HAMID *lifts him up and holds him tightly.*

AMIR: I can count to a hundred.

HAMID: Good boy, good boy.

JHILA *and* FATHER *watch.* AHMAD *tries to lift the imaginary* AMIR *away. The grown-up* AMIR *watches. The imaginary* AMIR *clings to* HAMID.

Please, Amir—be a good boy now. Let go.

The GUARD *pulls the* CHILD *away roughly.*

AMIR: [*to the* GUARD, *watching*] I hate you!

AHMAD: [*to the* CHILD] Shhh!

AMIR: Daddy! When I come back I will break all the locks. I will kill all them here and take you!

AHMAD *gives* AMIR *to the* GUARD, *who gives him to* JHILA. *The family moves off.*

AHMAD: [*lightly, taking* HAMID *back to his cell*] You should teach your son some discipline. You wasted your visit. You should have told her she won't get it better anywhere else. What's the matter? Don't you like women? [*To* KAMRAN] Sit down. Take off the shoes. All right, undo a lace. Let me see one lace undone. Go on!

He grabs KAMRAN *and throws him to the ground.*

Undo the fucking shoe!

HAMID: Get off him.

AHMAD *squares up to* HAMID.

AHMAD: What's it to you?

HAMID: You don't need his shoes.

AHMAD: So your wife can't get your blood up, but he can?

HAMID: Just leave him alone.

AHMAD: A woman like her—she needs it, you only have to look at her.

HAMID: What do you know?

KAMRAN: Hamid, leave it.

AHMAD: We watch her. At university. She's passed her exams all right. [*To* KAMRAN] I'll kick shit out of you later.

He moves away. Pause.

KAMRAN: I call him Hassan Gestapo.

HAMID: He's been taking the piss out of me since I got here.

KAMRAN: He does it to everyone.

HAMID: That's because everyone lets him get away with it.

KAMRAN: I'm grateful for what you did, but it was very stupid.

HAMID: I should have killed him.

KAMRAN: Listen to me, Hamid. We're living in a prison. If we don't live
by its rules we're finished. If you try and fight him he'll beat you
every time, because in this world he's king. But in here [*indicating
his head*] he's nothing, this place is nothing—this is the real world.

HAMID: My mind's like a desert.

KAMRAN: Mine too. But I've laid a carpet over all the sand and dust.
A miraculous carpet, of intricate beauty. [*He lies down, arms
outstretched.*] I lie on it and I'm lying in an eternal garden. I can
smell the clear water of its streams, feel the warmth of its peacock
feathers, see the red and yellow of its New Year flowers. [*He sits
up.*] And I'm king of this land! And it doesn't matter who goes to
war against it, who invades or occupies it—I still see it! The colours
of a good carpet never fade. Its beauty is indestructible.

HAMID: Well, the view from your head is better than the view from
mine. All I see is a man being treated like a dog.

KAMRAN: Why give them an excuse to kill you? You want to see your
wife again, don't you?

> HAMID *nods.*

Then think of other things. Don't make trouble.

> *Pause.*

HAMID: If you think that, why don't you give him your shoes?

KAMRAN: [*smiling*] I like them.

> *They laugh.*

♦ ♦ ♦ ♦ ♦

SCENE FIVE

Canberra. Brendan's office.

STEPHANIE: If Hamid wants to speak in court, you won't be able to stop
him. You'd have to take yourself off the case—

BRENDAN: It's what you want, isn't it?

STEPHANIE: That's one option. The other is that you start listening to
him.

BRENDAN: You mean to you.

STEPHANIE: Why does everything have to go your way or not at all?

BRENDAN: I'm all ears.

STEPHANIE: All right. The raid on the Mojahedin camp. They said fifteen hundred people were killed, didn't they? Only one person died.

BRENDAN: One? Why would the Iranian Government pretend to kill fifteen hundred people?

STEPHANIE: To encourage the hard-line Mullahs to vote for them.

BRENDAN: So the protest, and all this shit, happened for nothing?

STEPHANIE: The bombing, and all the fallout worked. The bastards were re-elected.

BRENDAN: So what have you got? Only one dead guy, a smashed-up Embassy—on camera—and a billion-dollar trade deal at stake. How are you going to get 'round that?

STEPHANIE: [*steely*] I don't think you're listening. [*Handing him a booklet*] Read that.

BRENDAN: What is it?

STEPHANIE: A Mojahedin magazine.

BRENDAN: It's propaganda.

STEPHANIE: It says there isn't an Iranian diplomat anywhere in the world who hasn't got blood on his hands. Apparently to qualify as diplomats they have to spend time in jail, as torturers. Iran knows if they try to defect, the country they're serving in won't take them. They're tied to the regime by blood.

BRENDAN: Okay. That makes sense. But why would they go out of their way to provoke a riot?

STEPHANIE: To embarrass the Australian Government.

BRENDAN: Stephanie…

STEPHANIE: [*with energy*] Listen. There's Ahmad sitting in the Embassy, expecting trouble, phones the police for help and they say no. The protesters turn up and get over-excited. But it's only a few straggling families. The embarrassment factor decreases. Unless Ahmad, as a secret aggressor, beefs it up when the camera's not looking. So it's conspiracy all right, but only between the governments and the Prosecution.

BRENDAN: And if you can't get the diplomats in court to cross-examine?

STEPHANIE: They're still on TV, in the papers, out for revenge. They'll be there!

BRENDAN: Suppose you can't get them?

STEPHANIE: That's the risk we take. The onus of proof isn't on us. We've tried it your way. It hasn't worked. We've got the gate, the door, the bin throwing, the concocted allegations of theft. What have we got to lose?

BRENDAN: Only the case.

STEPHANIE: Not if we get evidence to support what Hamid wants to say.

BRENDAN: All right. Prove it to me. Come on.

He gets up to go.

STEPHANIE: Where?

BRENDAN: The scene of the crime.

♦ ♦ ♦ ♦ ♦

SCENE SIX

Hamid's mind, then the Embassy in Canberra.

STEPHANIE *and* BRENDAN *walk to* KAMRAN, *as* HAMID *tosses and turns in a nightmare. They place* KAMRAN *on his knees and calmly walk to* AHMAD *and nod to him. He returns this acknowledgment and they move away.* AHMAD *beats* KAMRAN, *who remains impassive, as* HAMID *reacts to each blow in pain.* STEPHANIE *and* BRENDAN *examine the street outside the Embassy while the beating continues. After a few moments it ceases.*

STEPHANIE: This is where their cars were parked. This is where they ran.

BRENDAN: Hang on. There's a car.

A car passes them. BRENDAN *follows.*

STEPHANIE: Where are you going?

BRENDAN: The gate's still open. Come on. I know the bloke who's driving.

STEPHANIE: This is trespassing!

BRENDAN: I want to have a look at that door.

STEPHANIE: Brendan, we can't.

BRENDAN: Come on.

She darts through.

STEPHANIE: It's closing automatically. It didn't on the day.

BRENDAN: Okay, one up for Hamid.

STEPHANIE: How are we going to get out?

BRENDAN: Trust me.

STEPHANIE: Oh, shit.

BRENDAN: What are they going to do to us? We're just innocent defence lawyers getting a feel of the place.

The beating continues for a few moments until KAMRAN *collapses.* HAMID *startles awake.* KAMRAN *picks himself up.*

KAMRAN: [*to* HAMID] You're dreaming again.

HAMID: Kamran!

BRENDAN *sees* JOHN *approaching.*

BRENDAN: John, mate!

AHMAD *replaces his shirt and jacket.*

JOHN: Brendan—what the hell are you doing here?

BRENDAN: I was going to ask you that. You know Stephanie James?

JOHN: Hello.

He rings the bell of the Embassy. AHMAD *combs his hair.*

I'd make myself scarce, if I were you.

STEPHANIE: We're just going.

BRENDAN: What's the story?

JOHN: Compensation. For damage and injuries sustained. The Iranian Government's made a claim.

He rings the doorbell again as AHMAD *mops his brow with a handkerchief.*

BRENDAN: How much?

JOHN: Since it's you… four hundred thousand dollars.

AHMAD *approaches the door.*

BRENDAN: Bloody hell.

JOHN: The diplomat with the head wound's up for a quarter of it.

STEPHANIE: For a scratch!

JOHN: Ah, now don't be nasty—poor fellow's in trauma.

STEPHANIE: I bet he is.

> *The door of the Embassy opens.* AHMAD *smiles broadly, arranging his handkerchief in his top pocket.*

AHMAD: Ah, Mr Carter—welcome!

> *They shake hands.*

You've brought your colleagues along. How nice.

JOHN: And I'm afraid they've just been called back to the office.

AHMAD: What a pity. Perhaps you'd like some tea before you leave?

STEPHANIE: No—thank you. We'll be off now.

BRENDAN: Just a moment. Mr Husseini, I'd like to check something.

JOHN: Brendan.

BRENDAN: Won't take a second, John—you remember—that difficulty with the claim. There was a query, Mr Husseini, about this door. About whether or not it was possible for the protesters to have forced it open.

AHMAD: I don't understand. There is no doubt.

> *He shields the door.*

BRENDAN: May I look, Mr Husseini? The door is the same one, I presume?

AHMAD: What did you say your name was, Mr… er? Brenda?

> BRENDAN *is behind him.*

Do you mind, sir? I have not given permission—

JOHN: Mr Husseini and I have work to do, Brendan.

AHMAD: This man is truly a colleague of yours?

BRENDAN: Thanks for your patience, Mr Husseini.

AHMAD: [*looking* BRENDAN *in the eye*] Just who the hell are you?

BRENDAN: No need to get nasty.

AHMAD: Get out of here.

> *He grabs* BRENDAN'*s lapels and pulls him up.*

What do you think you are doing?

BRENDAN: I could ask the same of you, sunshine.

STEPHANIE: Let it go, Brendan.

AHMAD: I will find out what's going on here, you be sure of that!

JOHN: This is very embarrassing.

> *Pause.*

AHMAD: Yes.

> *He lets go of* BRENDAN.

Well, you have taken me by surprise today, you see. We are very nervous, very worried since the attack. However, it would be wise for you to go now.

BRENDAN: Yes. Well. Thanks, John.

> AHMAD *and* JOHN *enter the building.*

STEPHANIE: Bloody show-off.

BRENDAN: Haven't enjoyed myself so much in years.

STEPHANIE: What about the door?

BRENDAN: Solid as a rock.

STEPHANIE: Yes!

BRENDAN: Ahmad's not exactly a secret aggressor, is he? Went off like a firecracker.

STEPHANIE: Yeah… but if you've just ruined our chances of getting these bastards, I'll bloody kill you.

◆ ◆ ◆ ◆ ◆

SCENE SEVEN

The take-away shop.

JHILA *cashes up.* HAMID *plays the flute.* KAMRAN *sits nearby.*

AMIR: We had a letter from the bank today. We might have to sell the shop. Dad just looks after Kamran. So Mum's trying to hold it all together. [*With irony*] She paints Persian-style Aboriginal designs on boomerangs for some Iranian guy in Sydney.

JHILA: Oh, what's wrong with this?

> *She counts the notes again.* AMIR *walks by.*

Amir—don't drag your feet!

AMIR: All right, Mum. I get out of here as much as I can. Kamran staring, Mum stressing, Dad out of it. I can't stand it.

JHILA: Hamid, we're ten dollars down.

> HAMID *shrugs.*

Well?

HAMID: A woman came in today. She thought she had enough money—

JHILA: So you let her off paying?

HAMID: She had kids—they looked poor. What else should I have done, taken the meat out of their kebabs?

JHILA: You gave away food when we can hardly feed ourselves?

HAMID: Ten dollars is nothing.

JHILA: So why am I going out to work tonight?

HAMID: I don't ask you to.

> *He plays the flute.*

JHILA: Have you given up on this place?

> *He plays on.*

Will you listen to me!

> *She snatches the flute from him.*

Am I the only one—? Kamran, the back room—now, please.

> KAMRAN *stares at her.*

Now!

> *He goes, but eavesdrops on their conversation.*

HAMID: Don't speak to him like that, he's got his dignity.

JHILA: I'll speak to him any way I like!

HAMID: He's sick.

JHILA: Why are you so worried about him when you seem to hate each other so much? Was it something from in the prison? Everything that's happening to us starts and finishes there.

HAMID: I'm sorry.

JHILA: You care more about him than me. [*She hands back the flute.*] Here.

HAMID: That's not true.

JHILA: We're strangers. This silence between us isn't going to solve anything. It's like when Masud was with us. We nearly sacrificed everything for him, but I won't do it again.

She leaves. KAMRAN *hurries past* HAMID *with a suitcase.*

KAMRAN: I'm going.

HAMID: You can't.

KAMRAN: Jhila will get angry with you again.

HAMID: No she won't.

KAMRAN: The shop is closed. Jhila will get—I'm going.

HAMID: No.

KAMRAN: Don't tell me what to do!

HAMID: Unpack your case.

KAMRAN: Don't tell me what to do!

HAMID: Come on, my friend.

KAMRAN: You're no friend of mine. You betrayed me—

HAMID: [*overlapping*] I betrayed you.

KAMRAN: [*overlapping*] You betrayed me—

HAMID: [*overlapping*] I betrayed you… Have we said it enough times yet?

KAMRAN: [*overlapping*] You betrayed… I'm sick of the sight of your face.

HAMID: [*overlapping*] Shut up, will you…? When will you stop this?

KAMRAN: I'm sick of staring at your face.

HAMID: Oh, come on, you do it all day, you must like it!

KAMRAN: You're a traitor!

HAMID: No! I did what you taught me to do, you bastard! Give me that.

He snatches the case away.

It's empty again!

KAMRAN: I packed my everything.

Pause.

HAMID: I'm sorry.

KAMRAN: I don't want your sorrow.

He takes his case away. HAMID *buries his face in his hands.*

◆ ◆ ◆ ◆ ◆

SCENE EIGHT

Brendan's office.

STEPHANIE: [*answering the phone*] Brendan's phone... Yes, Peter...
No, he's gone to lunch... We visited the Embassy, yes... But...
But, Peter, I thought you were with me on this? We're so close to
getting the dirt on these guys... Why have you suddenly turned cold
on this? Who've you been talking to...? Foreign Affairs...? That's
ridiculous, they're bluffing... I beg your pardon...? What are you
trying to say...? I see... Of course I like it here... All right, Peter, I
get the picture... That would be nice, yes... Okay. 'Bye. [*She puts
the phone down.*] Shit.

    *She grabs some paper and hastily writes. She jumps when she
    sees* BRENDAN.

I was writing you a note.
BRENDAN: You dropping me?
STEPHANIE: What?
BRENDAN: It was a joke.
STEPHANIE: After your ridiculous behaviour this morning, Mr Husseini
phoned home, didn't he? So now we've got Foreign Affairs
breathing down our necks. Peter's livid. We're out of our depth,
Brendan. It's getting bloody dangerous. If we continue to hassle
these diplomats in or out of court, how can we protect the Parsis,
or their family in Iran? Thanks to you we're back to square one.
We can hardly cross-examine the diplomats with all guns blazing
now, can we? We'll have to play it straight down the line. And you
needn't look so pissed off. It's what you always wanted, and now
I've got no choice!
BRENDAN: Nice speech.
STEPHANIE: Do you think I'm playing games here, Brendan? You
fucked up.
BRENDAN: You're wasting your breath. The boys in Tehran have
ordered the diplomats off the case.
STEPHANIE: What?
BRENDAN: You didn't practise a speech for this eventuality? [*Pause.*]
Peter threaten your job, did he?
STEPHANIE: No.

BRENDAN: Come on…

STEPHANIE: Think what you like. [*Pause.*] What do we do now?

BRENDAN: I'm going to Brisbane. You fuck off and get your partnership.

STEPHANIE: Hang on a minute—

BRENDAN: Hey, Stephanie, you don't need to explain anything to me, okay? Just take a look at yourself. You're transparent.

Pause.

STEPHANIE: He didn't just threaten my job.

BRENDAN: It doesn't fucking matter now anyway, does it? The diplomats are out of it. The jury's denied half the evidence.

STEPHANIE: So why are you going to Brisbane?

BRENDAN: If Ahmad was a secret aggressor, why isn't Hamid falling over himself to point the finger at him? He's got to come clean about what he was doing with that bloody spanner. And what Kamran was up to.

STEPHANIE: I'd like to come with you?

BRENDAN: It's a free country.

♦ ♦ ♦ ♦ ♦

Caroline Kennison as Stephanie and Joss McWilliam as Brendan in the 1998 Matrix Theatre Company production at the La Boite Theatre, Brisbane. (Photo: Rob Maccoll)

SCENE NINE

Hamid's mind, then the take-away shop.

HAMID *sits, head in hands.* AHMAD *thrusts* KAMRAN *and three other* PRISONERS *against a wall, as* HAMID *is forced to watch. Three shots ring out, the* PRISONERS *fall.* KAMRAN *is left standing. A* GUARD *forces* KAMRAN *to his knees, pushing his legs apart.* HAMID *collapses. A* GUARD *(the actor playing* JHILA*) forces him to watch.* AHMAD *smashes the end of a bottle. Blackout.* KAMRAN*'s limp body is thrown down into a pool of red light.*

JHILA: [*still holding his head*] Hamid, Hamid. Come on, you've got to wake up. Come on, my love.

    They rest against each other.

HAMID: So much blood—you got to—the blood, he's dying—
JHILA: You're dreaming.

    He groans. She helps him up.

You sleep and have nightmares. I can't even sleep at all.
HAMID: It was the prison, but it was here. Kamran was—
JHILA: It's always Kamran.
HAMID: They made me—
JHILA: Yes?
HAMID: I can't—oh God, oh God… I've forgotten it all—it's going out of my head—
JHILA: That's what happens with dreams—
HAMID: This is real life.
JHILA: You're as mad as each other!
HAMID: [*looking around*] Where is he?
JHILA: Perhaps he needed a break from you?
AMIR: He's hiding from us again. I'm hoping he's gone for good. But we don't have time to look for him because Brendan and Stephanie turn up.
JHILA: [*to* AMIR, *in Farsi*] Be a good boy. Come back in an hour. Go water the roses.
HAMID: Keep an eye open for Kamran!

    BRENDAN *and* STEPHANIE *join* HAMID *and* JHILA.

AMIR: They're questioning Dad like the trial's tomorrow, like the police trying to trick a suspect. Then they ask him to remember the raid again. When the camera caught him with his arm raised.

BRENDAN: What happened before that moment?

HAMID: I don't know.

STEPHANIE: Who was nearby?

HAMID: I don't see anyone.

BRENDAN: Try to remember—

HAMID: Diplomat throw bin. I scared and see him want book—I tell you this many times.

BRENDAN: You think he's attacking you, you raise the spanner—

HAMID: Yes, and not hit.

JHILA: [*in Farsi*] Why are they asking you all this?

HAMID: [*in Farsi, angrily*] I don't know. [*In English*] I have no more to tell you. Nothing!

JHILA: [*in Farsi*] Calm down, Hamid.

HAMID: [*in Farsi*] Shut up!

JHILA: [*in Farsi*] You shut up!

AMIR: [*entering the shop*] Can I come in now?

JHILA: [*in Farsi*] Amir! I said one hour! Look, you've trodden mud in—how long have you lived in this family? Get out! Just get out.

AMIR: All right, Mum—all right! [*He goes to the back room.*] Call this a family?

HAMID: [*in Farsi*] Apologise to your mother!

STEPHANIE: I'm sorry, Hamid, we're still not clear about this. Did you see anyone else nearby when you were with the diplomat?

HAMID: I don't know.

BRENDAN: What about Kamran?

HAMID: I don't know where he is.

BRENDAN: No, where was Kamran when you were near the diplomat?

HAMID: I say no more!

BRENDAN: Did he see you with him?

HAMID: I don't know!

BRENDAN: Did he witness you attacking Husseini?

HAMID: I never attack I tell you!

BRENDAN: Did Kamran attack him?

AMIR: Mum! Dad!

They all run to see KAMRAN *lying in a pool of blood.*

STEPHANIE: Where's he cut?

JHILA: [*pointing to his wrists*] Hands—

STEPHANIE: Get some towels, quickly.

    JHILA *gets serviettes.*

Hamid, proper towels too.

    STEPHANIE *holds a pad on one arm,* JHILA *on the other.* HAMID *doesn't move.*

Brendan, you do it—hurry up!

JHILA: Cupboard by stairs.

    BRENDAN *goes.* AMIR *is transfixed.*

HAMID: I must do this—

    He tries to take *over from* STEPHANIE.

KAMRAN: [*in English*] Do not let him.

STEPHANIE: Hamid, I'm trying to stop the bleeding.

KAMRAN: [*in English*] I want bleed.

STEPHANIE: It's all right, Kamran. Hamid, let me, please.

KAMRAN: [*to* HAMID, *in Farsi*] Let me bleed.

BRENDAN: What's he saying?

STEPHANIE: It's okay. He cut himself the wrong way. It's only superficial, but he should have it looked at.

HAMID: I take him.

JHILA: [*in Farsi*] You've been drinking.

HAMID: [*in Farsi, to* KAMRAN] Please let me help you.

JHILA: I take him to medical centre in car—

HAMID: [*in English*] I take him.

KAMRAN: [*in Farsi*] No. Face what you've done.

BRENDAN: [*to* AMIR] What's he saying?

HAMID: [*to* KAMRAN, *in Farsi*] Why are you doing this?

AMIR: It's too fast.

KAMRAN: [*in Farsi*] If I live or die, you're guilty. I only stuck around to see you suffer.

AMIR: He says Dad's guilty if he lives or dies.

JHILA: [*in Farsi*] That's enough. Kamran, come on.

KAMRAN: [*in Farsi*] No! Tell them! You stopped me killing that bastard.

HAMID: [*clasping* KAMRAN *'s shoulders, in Farsi*] You said we shouldn't once. Kamran, please forgive me—

KAMRAN: [*in Farsi*] You killed me instead. Admit it!

HAMID: [*in Farsi*] I can't—please—

KAMRAN: Tell them! Tell them!

♦ ♦ ♦ ♦ ♦

SCENE TEN

The prison, Tehran.

HAMID *still holds* KAMRAN *by the shoulders, but they laugh a little and respond to the* GUARD.

GUARD: Shut up and sleep, you bastards!

> PRISONERS *are trying to sleep. Someone groans.*

PRISONER ONE: Shut up!

PRISONER TWO: My stomach.

HAMID: It's the bloody rice.

PRISONER TWO: Oh, God… [*Running to the door*] Please—open up— toilet, quick!

PRISONER ONE: Keep it down, will you?

HAMID: What's your problem?

PRISONER ONE: I'm trying to sleep!

HAMID: The guy's in trouble.

> PRISONER TWO *bangs on the door.*

PRISONER ONE: I don't give a shit!

HAMID: Keep your mouth shut.

PRISONER TWO: Where the hell are they? Come on!

PRISONER ONE: [*scrambling to his feet*] What did you say?

HAMID: I said keep your mouth shut.

PRISONER ONE: Right.

> *He starts to attack but groans and joins* PRISONER TWO.

Open up, for God's sake, open up!

> HAMID *laughs.*

AHMAD: What do you want?

PRISONER TWO: Open the door—we're sick.

AHMAD: Go back to bed.

PRISONER TWO: We're shitting ourselves in here!

AHMAD: Use the bucket.

KAMRAN: Hassan, it's Kamran. Please let them out.

> AHMAD *opens the door.*

AHMAD: Go on.

KAMRAN: Thank you.

AHMAD: I've done you a favour.

KAMRAN: You have.

AHMAD: So now I'll have the shoes.

KAMRAN: No.

> AHMAD *grabs* KAMRAN*'s throat, choking him.* HAMID *faces* AHMAD.

AHMAD: What are you going to do?

KAMRAN: Hamid. Please…

Errol O'Neill (left) as Kamran and Russell Dykstra as Ahmad in the 1998 Matrix Theatre Company production at the La Boite Theatre, Brisbane. (Photo: Rob Maccoll)

HAMID *helps* KAMRAN *up.* AHMAD *leaves.*

I'm going to give him the shoes.

HAMID: No you're not! Come on.

KAMRAN *winces.*

Are you all right?

KAMRAN: Are you?

HAMID: I'm thinking of other things.

KAMRAN *chuckles.*

Now lie down.

The sick PRISONERS *have returned.* HAMID *settles* KAMRAN *under his blanket. A fart resounds. Everyone laughs.*

Did you hear the one about the Frenchman, the Italian and the Iranian? Well. Death was doing his rounds one day, all in black, and he comes up to the three guys, and he says to them, 'It's time to die'. But none of them wants to go. So Death says, 'All right, I'm a reasonable man, each of you can ask me for one thing, and if I can't do it, you're free to live'. And they think, 'This guy's an idiot'. So the Frenchman says, 'Bring me the Eiffel Tower'— but lo and behold there it is, standing in front of him. 'Shit', says the Frenchman, and he's dead. Then the Italian says, 'Bring me the Leaning Tower of Pisa'. And there it is. 'Oh shit', he says, and he's dead. So Death turns to the Iranian. 'What do you want me to do?' he says. So the Iranian cocks his leg, goes [*making the sound of a fart*], smiles and says, 'Paint that!'

The PRISONERS *laugh.* AHMAD *and another* GUARD *enter. Everyone is quiet.* HAMID *continues to laugh momentarily. They stare at one another.* AHMAD *goes to kick* HAMID *but* KAMRAN *thrusts his shoes between them.* AHMAD *takes them.* KAMRAN *pulls his blanket over himself.* AHMAD *grinds* KAMRAN's *foot into the ground with his own.* AHMAD *stands in front of* HAMID, *imitating* HAMID's *earlier laughter.* HAMID *lowers his eyes.* AHMAD *leaves, lighting a cigarette. The* GUARD *remains at the door. A* PRISONER *tends to* KAMRAN. HAMID *is motionless.*

AHMAD: [*kicking the toilet door*] Get it over with.

He puts the cigarette in his mouth and moves away.

HAMID: [*going to the* GUARD] I've got the shits.

GUARD: Go on.

> AHMAD *places the baton on the ground and takes off his shoes in order to put on* KAMRAN's *good ones. He holds them up to admire them.* HAMID *comes up behind* AHMAD, *picks up his baton and hooks it under* AHMAD's *chin, holding it tightly against his throat.* AHMAD *tries to wrench the baton away.*

◆ ◆ ◆ ◆ ◆

SCENE ELEVEN

The take-away shop.

HAMID: [*still holding the baton against* AHMAD's *throat*] I held stick against his throat, and I could not kill. I ask myself a thousand times why not.

> HAMID *casts the baton to one side.* AHMAD *moves away.*

When I take off stick, he says, 'You are finished, you and friend!' Two days later he take us to room, with others, and does execution. Makes Kamran live and others die. Then—broken bottle, and me watching. And again I do nothing. [*To* AMIR] This is your brave father.

JHILA: [*in Farsi*] If you'd killed him, we wouldn't be together now.

HAMID: [*in Farsi*] You'd be better off.

KAMRAN: [*in Farsi*] Speak in English, so they can all hear it.

HAMID: [*in English*] I gave reason, Hassan Gestapo, to torture Kamran.

BRENDAN: You can't be sure of that.

HAMID: All excuses is shit, all is nothing, when I should have killed!

STEPHANIE: But there are excuses, Hamid.

HAMID: Is nothing of your business. You keep quiet, please. You don't know all. Story ends only in Embassy. Spanner is raised—

BRENDAN: What do you mean?

HAMID: Spanner is raised and again I cannot kill him—

KAMRAN: [*in Englis*h] Tell them who it is!

HAMID: I think—I think to myself—

KAMRAN: [*in English*] Who is it?

HAMID: I think it will make me bad like him—

KAMRAN: Who—?

HAMID: —Hassan Gestapo.

KAMRAN: Hassan Gestapo.

HAMID: Kamran knocks him down, to kill with screwdriver. For him revenge is everything!

KAMRAN: He stops me.

HAMID: I stop him.

KAMRAN: You betrayed me.

HAMID: [*to* KAMRAN] What did you teach me? [*Gesturing to his head*] Where's this beautiful place?

KAMRAN: Now, now you will find it.

JHILA: [*in Farsi*] Why didn't you tell me? Did you think I wouldn't love you anymore?

AMIR: You did the right thing, Dad.

STEPHANIE: Ahmad Husseini is Hassan Gestapo?

HAMID: It's not so amazing.

STEPHANIE: I suppose not. [*To* BRENDAN] If we hadn't gone to the Embassy, we could have cross-examined the bastard.

BRENDAN: I didn't think about it. I just ran in.

STEPHANIE: A moment of madness.

HAMID: Brendan. Maybe I win, maybe I lose, but I speak in court.

BRENDAN: Fair enough.

JHILA: Our lives are in hands of jury.

HAMID: You can go.

> STEPHANIE *and* BRENDAN *begin to move off.*

Brendan. You think I lose?

BRENDAN: Doesn't matter what I think, Hamid. You're the client.

> *Pause.*

AMIR: Dad's talking to us again. We keep trying to make him practise what to say in court, but he plays his flute instead. At least he's with us now. Mum told our neighbour she's got a new husband. Just like she did in Iran, when Dad got out of prison.

◆ ◆ ◆ ◆ ◆

SCENE TWELVE

The prison, Tehran / The court, Canberra.

Loud banging.

GUARD: Parsi. Get up! Your trial's on!

> HAMID *stirs.*

Hamid Parsi!

HAMID: I'm coming. Kamran? I've got my trial. Kamran?

GUARD: Parsi—

HAMID: I can't see. Kamran?

GUARD: Hurry up!

PRISONER: He's gone. They took him away.

GUARD: Shut up!

HAMID: When?

PRISONER: In the night.

> *The* MULLAH *begins to wrap his black turban.*

> *Canberra. The court.*

HAMID: Sorry we're late. We've got a problem. There's a guy waiting to go in. He's one of those diplomat people, he's got to be a spy— for Iranian Government, you know? He's got the… badge—

JHILA: Emblem—of Embassy—

HAMID: Whatever. Yes. On his case. If that guy tells Government in Iran what we say—it's no good for our family over there.

JHILA: If they have tape or camera.

BRENDAN: I'll get someone to look into it—come on.

STEPHANIE: You go in.

> *The* MULLAH *ties the end of his turban.*

> *Courtroom, Canberra. The* JUDGE *puts on his wig.* HAMID *is pushed centre stage by an Iranian* GUARD. BRENDAN, STEPHANIE *and* JHILA *sit nearby.*

BRENDAN: Your Honour, may I take this opportunity to thank the police for removing the Iranian Government spy this morning. My client further requests that the gentleman in the front row of the gallery, who appears to be using his briefcase as a camera, also be investigated by the police—outside.

JUDGE: Is there any other person causing offence to your client whom I should evict from the court while I'm at it, Mr O'Sullivan?

The MULLAH *takes his place in court.*

AHMAD: The trial of Hamid Parsi.

MULLAH: You are a member of the Mojahedin.

HAMID: No. I'm not—never.

AHMAD *hits* HAMID.

BRENDAN: Hamid has forged for himself a life like any Australian. He has never faced discrimination here. He is grateful to us for welcoming him. He found himself in a nation where citizens are free to protest at injustice and cruelty. In his case, through heightened emotion, the protest simply got out of hand, which Hamid readily admits and is sorry for.

HAMID: [*in Farsi*] I just want to lead my simple life, with my family— that's all I want to do.

AHMAD: Shut up.

He hits HAMID.

BRENDAN: It's not a life he takes for granted. It's not a life he would jeopardise under any circumstances, especially through the planning of a criminal act.

MULLAH: Was Masud Amini your contact with the Mojahedin?

HAMID: I just gave him a place to stay.

AHMAD *hits* HAMID.

BRENDAN: It's all too easy for us to lump in our Muslim defendant here, with the terrorist fanatics we all see on TV and abhor. He protested against what he perceived to be a terrorist act on a huge scale, the reported slaughter of fifteen hundred people who fought for the freedom of their homeland from tyranny—the same tyranny which promotes terrorism worldwide and which none of us can ignore if we write the 'wrong' book, or if we simply travel by air.

HAMID *nods at* BRENDAN.

AHMAD: [*as the* AUSTRALIAN PROSECUTOR] Objection, your Honour—
this is political rhetoric.

JUDGE: Objection sustained. Mr O'Sullivan, please restrict yourself
to the evidence. Members of the jury, I request you not to take
into account any political considerations not directly related to the
evidence in this case.

AHMAD *hits* HAMID.

There will be an opportunity soon for the defendant to make a
statement.

MULLAH: Name all Mojahedin traitors here in the prison.

HAMID: I can't.

AHMAD *hits* HAMID.

AHMAD: [*as the* AUSTRALIAN PROSECUTOR] Please just answer the
question.

HAMID: No one plan anything. Gate was open, one of us run inside. We
just follow. There was diplomat—

AHMAD: [*as the* AUSTRALIAN PROSECUTOR] Did you, as he states, and
as the video evidence suggests, attack this diplomat with a spanner
as your weapon?

HAMID: No, no—he lunge. I raise my arm like this, because I think
'He's attacking me'. I want to tell jury, this was the guy who was
my torturer—in Tehran jail. When I was there they blindfold me
and handcuff me twenty-four hours a day, you know?

AHMAD: [*as the* AUSTRALIAN PROSECUTOR] I'm sure we all sympathise
with your difficult imprisonment in Iran—

HAMID: In the daytime we are in cage, this big—and all night in box,
small as coffin, no air.

JUDGE: Ladies and gentlemen of the jury—

HAMID: That bloody man Ahmad—the diplomat—he is responsible for
the terrible prison—

JUDGE: May I remind you—

HAMID: —what they did to us—tortured Kamran for doing nothing—

JUDGE: —not to take into account any political considerations not
directly related to the evidence.

HAMID: —kept people there for years without trial—Ahmad tied my
hands—Ahmad slash my feet—he is one of them who beats and
executes people!

JUDGE: I ask the jury to disregard that last remark.

HAMID: That is what Mojahedin fights for—against these cruel—even in streets, women flogged, buried to neck and stoned, children slashed, if they sing at wedding, bride gets slashed—

STEPHANIE: Hamid, keep calm.

HAMID: —they are animals—worse than animals—

MULLAH: You are a traitor to the Islamic Revolution.

HAMID: No. I am not—

AHMAD: Shut up!

> *He hits* HAMID.

JUDGE: It's not the jury's task to place on trial the Iranian regime—

HAMID: If I don't tell the whole thing you can't understand my action.

JUDGE: The jury is solely required to decide if any of the defendants in this trial are guilty of conspiring with one or more of the others to commit criminal acts.

HAMID: But I must speak for my defence!

> AHMAD *hits him. He collapses.*

AHMAD: [*as the* AUSTRALIAN PROSECUTOR] Our country has separately responded to the accused in a sympathetic way by allowing them to come to live in this country as refugees.

> *During this speech* JHILA *lights a candle in front of a mirror.* AMIR *drapes it with tinsel and Christmas baubles.*

We are allowed to ask for some things in return. We are allowed to ask them not to use their presence here as an opportunity to seek revenge for what happened in their homeland. We are allowed to ask them to leave their national disputes behind them.

AMIR: [*taking* JHILA*'s hand*] We're standing on an embankment at the back of the court building, waiting for the prison van to come through. It's all concrete and patchy grass. I think, 'This might as well be Tehran, and Dad's being taken away from us again'. But then I think 'At least, here, I know he's going to come home'.

◆ ◆ ◆ ◆ ◆

SCENE THIRTEEN

A cell in the court.

BRENDAN: [*handing* HAMID *a rose*] Amir says it's for freedom. He wants you to have it. To make you believe they bloomed again, he said.

> HAMID *smiles and takes it.*

You all right?

HAMID: Yes. Jhila has my bag.

BRENDAN: It's in the van now.

HAMID: Where is Kamran?

BRENDAN: With Jhila. We're flying them back to Brisbane later.

HAMID: Good. Stephanie did good job for him. Not even suspended! If I keep mouth shut, I might be on that plane, yes? You still think I was wrong?

> BRENDAN *shakes his head.* STEPHANIE *enters.*

STEPHANIE: Brendan. Hamid. You're not going to believe this. [*She waves a scrap of paper.*] The trial is null and void.

BRENDAN: What?

STEPHANIE: I got it from a brother of one of the jurors.

> BRENDAN *takes it.*

Read it out.

BRENDAN: [*reading*] 'They are all as guilty as sin. Find them guilty and get out of there before Christmas.' Who wrote it?

STEPHANIE: The juror's wife.

HAMID: This note is good?

BRENDAN: It could overturn the verdict.

STEPHANIE: Jurors mustn't have contact with anyone about the case, not even family. He broke the rules.

HAMID: Juror's brother dobbed him in?

STEPHANIE: Yes.

HAMID: What a terrible brother to have.

STEPHANIE: He could turn out to be your best friend.

HAMID: So if we tell Judge about this, we do trial again?

BRENDAN: It'll have to be investigated.

HAMID: While I wait in jail, maybe my whole year?

STEPHANIE: I don't know—but that's not the point. It's another chance.

HAMID: For you.

STEPHANIE: Nowhere else in the world were the sentences as long as yours.

HAMID: They're not going to deport me.

STEPHANIE: You've been shafted. The jury was prejudiced, the Judge shut you up.

HAMID: I just shouted louder—they hear me—

STEPHANIE: I want to fight this.

HAMID: But I don't want to fight. I respect Australian justice system.

> STEPHANIE *scoffs.*

I do. If we do it all again, it could all turn out same. Or worse. Just because bad note is found, whole system is wrong? I don't think we could fight better.

STEPHANIE: You can't just accept it.

HAMID: Jhila is on suspended sentence and Kamran is not guilty. I have knowledge wife is safe. My son leads free life. I can endure one year in an Australian jail, okay? In my head, I practise living beautiful life for when I'm home. So forget this, yes?

> *He hands back the note.*

BRENDAN: [*smiling*] Mad Iranian bastard.

HAMID: Hey, I am real Australian now. I am convict!

> STEPHANIE *and* BRENDAN *shake hands with* HAMID.

STEPHANIE: Goodbye, Hamid. Good luck.

> *They move away.*

[*To* BRENDAN, *with some hesitation*] Peter's asked me to go for a drink. You want to come with us?

BRENDAN: No thanks.

> STEPHANIE *moves away.* BRENDAN *moves away in the opposite direction.* HAMID *remains centre stage, rose in hand. He slowly lies down, still clutching it. This is a distinct reflection of* KAMRAN *lying on his carpet earlier.*

JHILA: [*to* BRENDAN] People in there. They make decision. They do not know difference of freedom and prison. They ruin our life.

AMIR: It's not ruined, Mum. It'll be fine again when he gets back.

JHILA: What we did was all for lie. Not fifteen hundred dead, just one.

BRENDAN: One is enough.

JHILA: False news to all world for regime to win election. They just lie to get vote.

BRENDAN: All governments lie.

JHILA: Since revolution one hundred thousand they have killed. I throw bottle at photograph of black demon who started it. Now we are guilty, regime is not?

AMIR: There he is! Dad! Dad!

He waves. HAMID *stands up and waves back.*

HAMID: Don't worry, Amir. I'm thinking of other things.

AMIR: So am I, Dad!

HAMID: Merry Christmas and happy New Year!

AMIR: Merry Christmas, Dad!

JHILA: Merry Christmas, Hamid.

HAMID: See you soon, Jhila! This is happiest day of my life!

The lights fade to black.

THE END